We Who Are A

Joanna Russ was an American writer, academ... 1937 in New York City, she is best known for her satirical science fiction novel *The Female Man*. Over the course of a prolific career, she wrote many other novels, such as *Picnic on Paradise* and *On Strike Against God*, as well as essays, plays and non-fiction. Later in her career, she became increasingly active in the field of feminist science fiction scholarship, and her feminist literary criticism in works such as *How to Suppress Women's Writing* continues to be influential today. Joanna Russ is widely regarded as one of the finest science fiction novelists of the twentieth century. She died in 2011.

Naomi Alderman is the author of three novels: *Disobedience*, *The Lessons* and *The Liars' Gospel*. She has won the Orange Award for New Writers and the *Sunday Times* Young Writer of the Year Award, and each of her literary novels has been broadcast on BBC Radio 4's *Book at Bedtime*. She was selected for *Granta*'s once-a-decade list of Best of Young British Novelists, Waterstones Writers for the Future, and was mentored by Margaret Atwood as part of the Rolex Mentor and Protégé Arts Initiative. She presents *Science Stories* on BBC Radio 4, is Professor of Creative Writing at Bath Spa University and she is the co-creator and lead writer of the bestselling smartphone audio adventure app *Zombies, Run!*. She lives in London.

Hari Kunzru is the author of the novels *The Impressionist*, *Transmission*, *My Revolutions* and *Gods Without Men*, as well as a novella and a story collection. His writing has appeared in the *New York Times*, *Guardian* and *New Yorker*, among many other publications. He has won literary prizes including the Somerset Maugham Award and the Betty Trask Prize and was previously named one of *Granta*'s Twenty Best Young British Novelists. Hari Kunzru lives in New York and his next novel, *White Tears*, will be published by Hamish Hamilton in 2017.

We Who Are About To . . .

JOANNA RUSS

With introductions by
Naomi Alderman and Hari Kunzru

PENGUIN BOOKS

PENGUIN BOOKS

UK | USA | Canada | Ireland | Australia
India | New Zealand | South Africa

Penguin Books is part of the Penguin Random House group of companies
whose addresses can be found at global.penguinrandomhouse.com.

First published in the United States of America by the Wesleyan University Press 1976
Reissued with a new introduction by Penguin Books 2016
003

Set in 11/13 pt Bembo Book MT Std
Typeset by Jouve (UK), Milton Keynes
Printed and bound in Great Britain by Clays Ltd, Elcograf S.p.A.

A CIP catalogue record for this book is available from the British Library

ISBN: 978-0-241-25374-8

www.greenpenguin.co.uk

MIX
Paper | Supporting
responsible forestry
FSC® C018179

Penguin Random House is committed to a
sustainable future for our business, our readers
and our planet. This book is made from Forest
Stewardship Council® certified paper.

Introduction

by Naomi Alderman

What a writer Joanna Russ is! How necessary her work is and how quickly it has fallen into half-neglect!

Of course, Russ herself might have predicted that she'd suffer a period of dormancy; she was astonishingly clear-eyed about women's lives and the subtle devaluing of women's work. Across her writing, she understood how women are belittled, pushed about, subjugated; and as she shows in *We Who Are About To . . .*, she knew as well that oppressed people necessarily end up with an impulse to strike first, strike hardest, take no prisoners.

For a slim volume, the concerns of *We Who Are About To . . .* are almost endless: the novel debates the nature of adventure, the future of travel, the advisability of medically-prolonged life, what it's like to pay for sex or be paid for it, whether there is a 'state of nature' for humanity and, finally, whether there can be a 'right way' to die.

Russ knew the 1960s-style SF masculine space cowboy epic like the back of her hand; this novel subverts it in a dozen different ways. Like the visionary futurist Stanisław Lem, Russ is uninterested with the hows of the new world. Not for her the elaborate descriptions of interstellar hyperdrives or warp engines. Instead, she wants to know how it will feel to land on a new world, how the old dynamics of human personality and inter-relations will play out in the future we're catapulting ourselves toward.

And, overturning our comfortable story of 'progress', Russ sees the future as continuous with the past; human beings don't change, we just invent different tools. Like Ballard, she turns our heads towards uncomfortable truths about ourselves: how long would we remain anything like ourselves without food, without water, without the rule of law, without sex? In her masterful early work *Picnic on Paradise*, Alyx, an assassin, is time-scooped from her birthplace among the ancient Phoenicians to escort a group of rich tourists off a snow-bound planet that's been caught up in an inter-galactic war. Russ's ideas are always bonkers, always brilliant.

Russ is also astonishingly prescient in her depiction of people of the future travelling constantly with mood-tweaking drugs. She predicts a world where people are afraid to feel; or perhaps she saw that people have always been afraid to feel, and saw correctly that pharmaceuticals were increasingly giving us a way to numb, sup-press, turn off, tune out. But then: how much should we have to feel? How much suffering are we obliged to endure for the sake of this questionable good: our humanity?

Some novels point us towards other writers; Russ's work can certainly do that, *We Who Are About To . . .* directs us to references as diffuse as *The Swiss Family Robinson* and *The Cold Equations*. But a taste of Russ's work just gives us a hunger for more of her. Her concerns are as urgent now as they've ever been; more so. Her 1979 list of retorts to complaints about her fantasy-book review-ing could have been written today. 'You're vitriolic', said her attackers; Russ concurred: 'critics tend to be an irritable lot'. 'Just tell me what I'd enjoy reading', they demanded; 'bless you, what makes you think I know?' she replied mildly. And, just like today's internet trolls and haters, Russ's detractors complained: 'Don't shove your politics into your reviews' . . . 'I will,' she replied, 'when authors keep politics out of their books.'

Russ never kept politics out of anywhere. That's what makes her essential today.

Introduction

by Hari Kunzru

You've heard this one before. A motley group of travellers crash-lands on an alien planet. How will they survive? There are tensions between them. Who will emerge as the hero? Who will 'get the girl'? It's always the same story. And it's always the same hero: the young able-bodied white man who stories are always about, the dude who's so used to being Kirk in a world of redshirts that he imagines it's natural for everyone else to play supporting roles in his personal space-age psychodrama.

Except this is a book by Joanna Russ. Most famous for *The Female Man*, a novel that uses another old genre trope – parallel universes – to ask questions about gender and power, Russ is one of the most important writers of science fiction's seventies New Wave. Her pulp warrior heroine Alyx is an ancestor of Katniss Everdeen and Brienne of Tarth. Her sarcastically titled essay *How to Suppress Women's Writing* is a taxonomy of the ways that writing by women is marginalized and belittled. 'She didn't write it. She wrote it but she shouldn't have. She wrote it but it isn't art . . .' So it's no surprise that *We Who Are About To . . .* isn't another novel about *that* dude. In fact, from the bleak first page, where the unnamed female narrator announces that 'we're nowhere, we'll die alone', it's clear that Russ wants to talk to us about all those other books, all those episodes of all those shows where the usual archetypes (the 'professor', the hunk, the rich couple, the pretty girl) play the usual roles, with the usual oh-so-happy ending.

Even if the main furniture of the marooned-in-space genre is the Crusoe-esque business of survival – what will we eat? how will we repair our ship? – it always ends up being about social and political organization. Do we cooperate or strike out on our own? Do we sacrifice ourselves for others or look out for number one? Who gives the orders and what is done to those who disobey? Russ's answers to these questions are not the stuff of feel-good fantasy. Her take on the social dynamics of the shipwrecked survivors focuses on what happens to a dissenter, someone who doesn't agree with the consensus. If 'society', even a tiny society, decides that your body and your labour should be used for the good of the group, your resistance is a threat to the continued compliance of others. It must be crushed.

Russ's narrator dares to question the need for survival and colonization, for 'planning, power, inheritance'. She wants to live – and die – in her own way. When it was first published in 1977, *We Who Are About To . . .* made a lot of people uncomfortable. It doesn't say what people want to hear: that the human spirit will win through against all the odds, that deep down people are kind and good. Instead it does what the best SF ought to do, using speculation to unsettle and challenge, to strip away tired preconceptions and ask us to see our own world anew.

About to die. And so on.

We're all going to die.

The Sahara is your back yard, so's the Pacific trench; die there and you won't be lonely. On Earth you are never more than 13,000 miles from anywhere, which as the man said is a tough commute, but the rays of light from the scene of your death take little more than a tenth of a second to go . . . anywhere!

We're nowhere.

We'll die alone.

This is space travel. Imagine a flat world, a piece of paper, say, with two spots on it but very far apart. If you were a two-dimensional triangle, how would you get from one spot to the other? Walk? Too far. But fold the paper through the third dimension (ours) so that the spots match exactly – if you were a triangle you couldn't see or feel this, of course – and you *are* at the proper place. We do this in the fourth. Don't ask me how. Only you must be very, very careful, when you fold spacetime, not to sloosh the paper around or let it slide: then you end up not on the spot you wanted but God knows where, maybe entirely out of our galaxy, which is that dust you see in the sky on clear nights when you're away from cities. The glittering breath of angels. Far, far from home. The light of our dying may not reach you for a thousand million years. That ordinary sun up there, a little hazy now at noon, that smeary spot.

We do not know where we are.

At dawn there was an intensely brilliant flash far, far under the horizon, and about an hour later the noise of the thing; I figured the way you do for thunderstorms, the lag between light and sound: one-hippopotamus, two-hippopotamus, three-hippopotamus, four-hippopotamus, five-hippopotamus – there's your mile. Seven hundred miles. That's over a thousand kilometers. In the event of mechanical dysfunction, the ship's computer goes for the nearest 'tagged' planet, i.e. where human life is supposed to be possible, then ejects the passenger compartment separately. Lays an egg, you might say. We won't be visited without a distress call, however, now the colonization fever's died down (didn't take long, divide five billion people by twenty and the remainders start getting clubby again).

Goodbye ship, goodbye crew, goodbye medicine, goodbye books, goodbye freight, goodbye baggage, goodbye computer that could have sent back an instantaneous distress call along the coordinates we came through (provided it had them, which I doubt), goodbye plodding laser signal, no faster than other light, that might have reached somewhere, sometime, this time, next time, never. You'll get around to us in a couple of thousand years.

We're a handful of persons in a metal bungalow: five women, three men, bedding, chemical toilet, simple tools, an even simpler pocket laboratory, freeze-dried food for six months, and a water-distiller with its own sealed powerpack, good for six months (and cast as a unit, unusable for anything else).

Goodbye, everybody.

At dawn I held hands with the other passengers, we all huddled together under that brilliant flash, although I hate them.

O God, I miss my music.

(This is being recorded on a pocket vocoder I always carry; the punctuation is a series of sounds not often used for words in any language: triple gutturals, spits, squeaks, pops, that kind of thing. Sounds like an insane chicken. Hence this parenthesis.)

Of the women: myself. A Mrs Valeria Graham, actually married to Mr Graham, in the delicate fifties when alimony becomes mandatory upon divorce (who would pay whom is a conjecture here). Valeria Victrix habitually wears the classical Indian sari, usually gold embroidered on royal blue, like a television hostess's; this does not suit a petite chemical blonde. Ditto the many-splendored earrings: bells within cages within hoops.

A dark young woman who does yoga on her head, off to some 'unimportant job' somewhere (she said), hates everyone, says she's called Nathalie. Nathalie what? Nathalie nothing. Mind your own business.

Cassie, thirty-ish, beginning to put on weight; you'll find her waiting table in any restaurant or nude bar on any world. She looks like an earlier stage in the life-cycle of Mrs Graham, but that's an illusion; nothing but a convulsion of nature could let either of these two rise or fall to the other's level. (Hydrogen fusion, which provided unlimited power and should've made us all rich, but of course didn't.)

A Graham child, female, twelve, a beautiful café-au-lait so she is either Mrs Graham's by a former marriage or Mr Graham's ditto, or neither. Hors de combat all trip with one of the few bacterial diseases left, or rather the treatment for it, which had made her dreadfully ill. We'd see her only when she'd stagger into the lounge, looking beautiful and hopeless, and then vomit (again). For whoever finds this and has no Greek, an iatrogenic disease is one created by the physician and we have plenty of them. The physicians and the diseases.

This will never be found.

Who am I writing for, then?

The men: Mr Graham, a big powerful male in his early fifties, hollow and handsome in the same style as his wife: coloring, dress, and person. Three days out (we were on the way to find the first spot we can then fold on to the second spot) Cassie took off the mask, stopped being squeezably-soft, and lost all expression. The Grahams stopped speaking to her. I say 'male' because he emphasizes it subtly, so perhaps she's the buyer and he's the bought. Or both: money marries money. Relations with men are still apt to be patterned on a few rather dull models, especially among strangers, so I know less about the men than I do about the women, but in one way I know more: I mean the conception of themselves they find it publicly necessary to live up to.

Alan: a young man with a set of shoulders like unto those of

3

one who plays *le futbol* (says he did). Extremely polite and attentive, with a carefully intent way of listening to everybody and agreeing civilly and much too often ('Oh, I do agree with you, Mr Graham, I really do'). My theory is that this obviously insincere behavior conceals absolutely nothing; he's rich enough to take the poor man's Grand Tour, poor enough to need a job, decent enough not to hurt anyone unless he's frightened or hurt himself (which could happen pretty easily), and anxious enough to flatter whoever he thinks can help him. The Grahams, you see, are slumming.

An historian of ideas traveling from one University to another and extremely evasive about his work, as they all are, now there's so little of it to go around; he wears Mr Graham's kind of conservative clothes: shorts and sport-shirts, bright but not daylight-fluorescent (Vic Graham in blue, John Ude in red). The only historical analogy to Alan's costumes is Graustark, all gold braid, epaulettes, and boots (except the shako, which I think he had to leave behind on account of the weight, though he never mentioned it). The professor is John Ude. Thirties. A very minor intellectual. Bland. Often displays The Smile. The first day, in the lounge, when Mrs Graham actually introduced herself as *Mrs Graham* — which is rather like presenting yourself as a Dame of the British Empire or a Roman Tribune — Professor Ude displayed (after a blank moment) The Smile. Then he took out from his sporran The Pipe, gesturing at The Pipe with The Smile to show that he was aware of his own self-mockery. He would have received Valeria as Mistress Anne Bradstreet, had she so required, because the Grahams are rich. Black-body-suited, perpetually angry Nathalie said audibly, '*Missiz*! Oh God,' and turned away with an unbelieving, outraged, I-knew-it-was-going-to-be-one-of-those-trips look. Alan gaped hysterically, then shut his mouth. I said nothing. Think of it: Valeria and Victor in blue, Ude in red, Alan indescribable, Cassie in two stars and a cache-sexe (both silver), and Lori Graham in body paint, mostly blue (to match her parents' clothes). The arrows of Professor Ude's irony point only down in the social scale, never up; when they occasionally point at himself, he is very careful to blunt them.

4

Oh, we are a dull bunch! The professor once uncrimped enough to get into a long discussion with Victor Graham about the new lease on life given capitalism by the unlimited power of hydrogen fusion, the poor fool. He believes in free enterprise, competition, achievement-orientation, the meritocracy. He's never been behind the crew panels where the technocrats live. Travel enough and you can make friends with the crew, what's this, what's that, ask questions; they even let you fiddle about in sick bay if you're careful. You see things, then.

Meritocracy? We're being kept off the streets, that's all, rich or poor. (Foundations pay me to lecture on music and play tapes of it; that's why I travel. I'm a scrounge.)

I once said to Ude, 'How fast do you think things really change?'

He said, 'That's not my field.'

Cassie, determined, bitter, exhausted, full-breasted, wanted to know what a musicologist was and what kind of music.

'Very old,' I said. 'European twelfth century to Baroque. No farther.'

'How nice,' Mrs Graham said. 'We must tell Lori.'

'Who cares,' Cassie said.

I wear body-suits and sandals, like Nathalie, and keep a low profile, especially with passengers. This isn't a luxury liner; you don't have to eat with anybody, just dial a meal out of the locker.

And visit the crew. And envy them.

Behold the new irrelevants: parasites, scum, proles, scroungers. People who do nothing real.

No, dinosaurs.

Isn't . . . wasn't, I mean, a luxury liner.

Stranded dinosaurs.

Day first. I'm sitting in the corner on the empty tool chest after a little nap. Already excited talk of 'colonization,' whatever that is. Our tiny laboratory tells us the air is safe, although perhaps a little thin; there's nothing directly poisonous outside. Nathalie's unexpected talent for cataloguing and arranging tools (which is why the tool box is empty). The sun up for at least fifteen hours, taking a slow tour of the horizon at what my childhood tells me is four p.m. late autumn, so we have either a very great axial tilt or are in very high latitudes. A few weeks' observation and perhaps we can guess if we're approaching the summer solstice or going the other way, which could give us some idea of how long the seasons will be: could be ten years of summer (and it's hot outside now, about 30° C, they tell me). Through the window you can see ordinary green trees, hilly up-and-downish but not much, some little natural clearings. Very much like New Jersey a hundred and thirty-five years ago, when my ancestors came to Ellis Island: about nineteen-aught-five that was. My maternal something-great-grandfather was a plumber, my maternal something-great-grandmother a sheitel-maker. (A sheitel is a wig which Orthodox Jewish women used to wear after marriage, over their shorn hair. But what do you care.) We don't remember the actual genealogy of the other side nearly so far back, but I've inherited their looks; little, dark, Sephardic Jews fleeing the Spanish frontier at night with rubies, emeralds, and uncut diamonds sewn into the hems of their cloaks. At least I like to think of them that way. I carry the modern equivalent, the only currency that passes everywhere, sewn into my jacket, my neckband, my belt, so flat you couldn't detect it. I mean a whole pharmacopoeia. Because you never know what you will need. (I filched a little from the ship, too: nothing important.)

Our equipment isn't good enough to test whether the life here is edible. We're not supposed to do that. Commonly the problem has been people contaminating the planet, but there have been striking instances of vice-versa. We're supposed to stay inside.

Everybody is getting on everybody else's nerves.

Victor, in his hearty, overemphasized, hollow voice: 'I believe I should.' (Tail end of a conversation about who's to go out first. Not that it matters. We either go out eventually or cut our throats.)

'Why?' says Nathalie instantly.

'Because I'm old. Expendable. Why else?' (Lori Graham is looking adoring and anxious.)

'Very sensible,' says Nathalie. 'So should Mrs Graham.' (Lori outraged.)

'Well, if there's any harm . . .' This is John Ude.

'The Grahams will go,' says Nathalie over her shoulder, and continues putting together our shovels, our hammers, our axes – 'half an hour, no less, no more' – and something longer that comes in sections.

The Grahams go out the air-lock, Victor stooping, Alan kindly restraining Lori when she tries to slip out with them. They have an intense, whispered conversation, with Lori close to tears.

'My, you *are* just an ordinary traveler, aren't you!' I say to Nathalie, hoping to get a rise from her, maybe learn something. No answer. She's engaged in jointing together what we both realize at the same instant is a single-passenger hovercraft: sealed motor, no cab, kicks up so much dust that you have to wear an air-filter (included in the box; by Saint George, I was right), flies over any terrain with ease, including water (at under 32 kph, however), and looks like nothing so much as a stick with a saddle; hence its name.

'A br –' (she catches herself).

'Broomstick,' I finish. On her knees, in the midst of spare parts, in her black skin-tights, Nathalie gives me (for a moment only) a glance of shock, of wild surmise – *are you one, too?*

'Where were you really going?' I say.

She inspects her fingernails, comes to a quick decision, licks her lips wolfishly.

'Government trainee,' she says in a low voice but so naturally, that is to say pretend-naturally, that Cassie (who is lying on a bunk, holding to one ear a cheap, battery-powered music library that will wear out within days, I can tell) can't hear us.

'At what?' say I.

'Doesn't matter,' she says sharply. 'Not to tell. And I shan't now, not because it matters but because it doesn't.'

For a moment she's a death's-head.

7

Then 'What!' says Lori Graham, a little desperately, with the natural irritation of someone whose Mummy and Daddy may, after all, have been eaten by megatheria. 'Nothing,' answers Nathalie. 'Go on screwing with Alan or whatever it is you were doing.' (Lori makes a disgusted face and Alan turns aside to blush or giggle.) 'If he can,' she adds. In the low, trained voice she says to me, 'Who are you?'

'A musicologist,' I say. 'Sorry. Nobody like you. I've picked things up because I've traveled a lot, that's all.'

Cassie sits up, shaking her *radio*. She says to Nathalie, 'Can you do something with this thing?'

'The batteries are worn down and they're electric; we can't recharge them. You've been playing that ever since we started this trip and you've probably played it before, quite a lot. I know you've recharged them but the case is worn. So that's probably two hundred hours and a couple of rechargings; they do deteriorate each time, you know. And there's nothing we can do – our gadgets are all sealed and shielded. It's a different kind of energy; we can't transform the one to the other. Besides if we tried opening any of the powerpacks, we'd probably go boom, you know, just like the ship.' This is me. I add, 'I'm awfully sorry, Cassie.'

'So if you're a goddamn music student,' says Cassie at her most insulting, 'where's your goddamn music, huh?'

I'm tempted to answer 'in the ionosphere' (reduced to its constituent atoms, or even smaller pieces) but I say, 'It was in the baggage compartment.'

'Oh,' says Alan, clearly disappointed. I guess he has been planning on hearing some music. Cassie draws up her knees in the bunk, exasperated, and presses the side of her face against the sealed window.

Alan adds in a friendly way, 'Hey, don't you have any of it with you?' Forgetting to be polite, that one.

'Tapes,' I say. 'Want to use them for ribbons? I have the amplifier and the recorder – see? they fit in my hand – but the speakers are too big. Two meters diameter.'

He opens his mouth, probably to inquire why a speaker has to be two meters across, but Lori – who is *very* well educated, as her parents have been telling us for three weeks – breaks in importantly with a disquisition on the physical reproduction of sound, and how the lowest musical note that can be heard by the human ear is fourteen cycles per second and the lowest sounds that can be felt are even lower, and if you want a really good bass, say for Bach's Toccata and Fugue in D Minor for Organ, or Vestal's Electronic Mass, you just have to have these enormous speakers for your sound environment because otherwise the sounds just won't fit mechanically on the speakers. 'Literally,' she says.

'O-o-oh,' says Alan in mock awe.

Cassie breaks in furiously with, 'Your goddamn education –'

(John Ude has been asleep all this time, worn out, poor man; that's why you haven't heard from him.)

Thank God the Grahams come back in. The air-lock jams. We are now testing the atmosphere just as much as they, something Mr Ude (waked by the noise of Lori's rejoicings and questionings) seems to notice, but nobody's going to call attention to such things in the presence of an hysterical twelve-year-old with the habit of psychosomatic vomiting. (Her Momma says.)

Joy all around.

(I'm not, of course, recording this at the time it happened. I stole half an hour from the long, long dawn. Two and a half hours of twilight, then three more of real dark, and again two and a half hours of dusk-turned-backward: slow, creeping, endless, unadvancing grey.)

We're very high on the world's shoulder. Labrador perhaps. Even within the Pole circle. If the sun goes lower, if it sets closer to the place of its rising, if the dark shrinks, if red-sunset evolves without darkness into red-sunrise. Is this spring? Summer? Fall? We might be heading into a ten-month summer, a twenty-year summer. Desert? Everything dead, brown, burned? Think anyway of midwinter with the sun even lower and only three hours of daylight out of twenty-eight. A night twenty-five hours long.

In the brief, black, real dark we all went outside to look at the sky. A shiver of the nerves as the night air struck us, a kind of blind claustrophilia, wishing to get back into our own, closed-in, stale smell, away from the living odors of night coolness. Everyone stayed together. Black velvet, must be overcast; this awful sense of being outside. Vast space.

We looked up.

Nothing.

I mean there was almost nothing in the sky: a few bright stars near the zenith and halfway to the equatorial horizon a far, faint, dim blur. Island universes. From anywhere on Earth (they say) you can see about three thousand stars with the naked eye. You can also see that arch of powder which we call the Milky Way; it's the center of the galaxy. We're located in one of its arms; it's a kind of flattened ellipse. From anywhere near any galaxy, unless one is very far above or below its major plane, and in the wrong hemisphere to boot, you ought to be able to see something. Not that it matters, of course, for space travel. Still. Nothing matched the star maps Nathalie had (she would!) but then on the other side of the Equator, who knows? And none of us is very good at this sort of thing. But six stars and a blur . . . which might be, God knows, the Crab Nebula or our own, or unidentified astronomical object number goodness-knows-what, something so far away that (as I said) the light of our dying will reach you (whoever you are) only after you yourselves are long dead, after your own Sun has engulfed you and then shrunk to a collapsed cinder with no more light in it than what we saw that night.

Whoever, wherever, whenever.

Lori cried in her mother's arms. Mrs Graham very clumsy at comforting her daughter, perhaps always was. John, the professor of the history of ideas, saying something like 'Uh!' low, a sort of groan.

That empty.

Well, we might be visited in a routine check of the tagged worlds in as little as a couple of centuries, a century, eighty years even. Even little Lori will be dead.

John Ude said, 'Come on now, come on, dears. It's a tagged planet. It has to be. Too much coincidence otherwise, eh? The air, the gravity. Now if it's tagged, that means it's like Earth. And we know Earth. Most of us were born on it. So what's there to be afraid of, hey? We're just colonizing a little early, that's all. You wouldn't be afraid of Earth, would you?'

Oh, sure. Think of Earth. Kind old home. Think of the Arctic. Of Labrador. Of Southern India in June. Think of smallpox and plague and earthquakes and ringworm and pit vipers. Think of a nice case of poison ivy all over, including your eyes. Status asthmaticus. Amoebic dysentery. The Minnesota pioneers who tied a rope from the house to the barn in winter because you could lose your way in a blizzard and die three feet from the house. Think (while you're at it) of tsunamis, liver fluke, the Asian brown bear. Kind old home. The sweetheart. The darling place.

Think of Death Valley . . . in August.

Day two. It began. I just couldn't keep my damned mouth shut. Everybody running around cheerily into the Upper Paleolithic. We're going to build huts. We're going to have a Village Fire that Lori Graham will tend because she is the Fire Virgin or something. Mrs Graham is suddenly person-of-least-value. Victor says, 'Excuse me, dear,' with immense firmness and then goes about his business. He's going to go somewhere with John Ude to search for water. They won't drink it, of course, but will carry back samples and then we will analyze it, which is impossible because we don't have the equipment. But it will certainly help the water-distiller; our tanks are almost empty. Mrs Graham has suddenly become very cuddly with Lori, who keeps squirming away, saying, 'Valeria, *please*!' With twenty-five hours of daylight there's no rush, and besides we have to move everything outside (to find out if that will kill us). Outside it goes, mattresses and bedding (to get rained on or infested), tools and toolkit, all of this superficially showing immense order but in fact about as rational as the ooze of algae from a pond. Our nice, destructible laboratory (like litmus paper, use it once and it's done for) has told us that the sun will not burn us, although it has a small amount of ultraviolet, and more than the usual infrared (too low in the sky, anyhow); that the local vegetation does not contain mineral poisons; that the (local) air does not, either; and that the gravitation is 0.93, which is so close to terrestrial as makes no difference.

Nathalie's digging experimental sanitation pits with a collapsible shovel. And every once in a while it does.

I seek out Ude, who's unpacking the first-aid kit, and say, 'Benzedrine and bobby-pins!' but the joke's too old for either of us to have ever heard it, and too vulgar, base, and popular for him to have ever read it.

I say, 'Look, you've got an anti-pyretic, two wide-spectrum antibiotics, pain-killers, and a nice little pamphlet about how to make a splint out of a bunk-rail. *It's not enough.*'

'We'll make do,' he said heartily, flashing The Smile.

I said, 'My God, man, what will you do when Lori's wisdom teeth come in?' and the child, who must have clairaudience (she was a good five meters away) instantly emitted a nervous 'What!' and came over to join us. She had been watching Alan Bobby Whitehouse ponder about trying to start to learn to just possibly swing an axe without cutting his own foot.

'Your impacted wisdom teeth,' I said. '*Everybody* gets impacted wisdom teeth. I'm the only adult I know whose wisdom teeth came in straight. Of course I had gingivitis, and dental surgery, and fillings, and your mother has transplants. So where are we going to get all this?'

'Huh?' said Lori.

'They might just lie there for years,' I said. 'I know someone who didn't get them until they were thirty. On the other hand, you might have intense pain for a month before they die and rot inside your gums and take a couple of molars with them, which Daddy can knock out with a rock.

'O pioneers,' I added rather sourly.

'Now come on,' said John Ude.

(Funny. Everyone's around us now. I've attracted a crowd. The old raise-the-voice bit. And I wasn't even thinking of it.) I said, 'I don't want to make a speech —'

'Then don't,' said Cassie, who's been flapping our linens in the breeze just to make sure we get a nice dose of the local pollens.

'Well, fuck you then!' I said. 'I will.'

And I did. I must have talked for five or six minutes. I told them (and more):

That a tagged planet is not colonizable but means only bearable gravity, a decent temperature range, and air that won't kill you.

That survey teams sample only one square kilometer of a planet, doubtless not this one.

That there were no mineral poisons, but that we couldn't test for organics or allergens.

That there could be incompatible proteins, vitamin deficiencies, chelating agents, dozens of things that could mess us up biologically in dozens of ways.

That if we could eat the local macro-life, the local micro-life could eat us.

That we could die of exposure in the winter because we had no way to make heat after our bungalow wore out and that was in six months.

That we could die of heat in a summer whose length we didn't yet know.

That a breech birth could kill. That a three-days' labor and no dilation could kill. That septicemia could kill.

That heart failure could kill.

That none of us could even recognize flint, let alone know what to do with it.

That plastic was a lousy building material.

That each of us carried five to eight lethal genes, and that even without them, humanity had not exactly been breeding for survival for the past hundred years.

That there weren't enough of us.

And more. So much more.

I stopped. Too much of the old stiff-necked pride coming back. Giant Alan Bobby, with his axe, says, 'I think you better go on,' and I only hope Nathalie's training has included eye-gouging and larynx-smashing because this boy is beginning to find out – in two days! – that we are far, far from any law. I hope he can be shamed. I said:

13

'Well, I hope we find volcanic glass, because I could recognize that; I saw it once in a museum.'

This falls flat.

'What do you suggest we do?' says the Professor, with The Smile. 'You seem to think we have no chance.' Humor her.

I nodded.

The professor repeated, 'Just what do you suggest we do?'

Silence.

'Well, anything you please,' I said. 'Only leave me out of it.'

'That,' says Nathalie, 'will make three women and two men, if we exclude Victor, which puts the numbers considerably lower, doesn't it?'

'Jesus,' I said; 'Oh Jesus Christ, I'm forty-two years old. Do you think I can have my first child now? Besides you don't want me; my father was a bleeder.'

'Liar,' says Nathalie. 'I saw your medical records. You're not the only one who can get past the crew doors.'

'All right,' I said. (Nathalie the leader. Wait 'til Alan finds out he can beat you up.) 'All right, so you think you have the chance of a snowball in hell. Maybe you do. But *I* think that some kinds of survival are damned idiotic. Do you want your children to live in the Old Stone Age? Do you want them to forget how to read? Do you want to lose your teeth? Do you want your great-grandchildren to die at thirty? That's obscene.'

Here the ground came up and hit me, as it always does when you get carried away; it was Cassie, standing over me and shouting, 'Shut up! Shut up, you!' I don't think she hit me, only pushed. I wasn't ready, that's all. Rabble-rousing that used to work, but that doesn't work now because it's the wrong rabble and the wrong rouse. Well, we all know that.

And in everyone's face the flash of realization: no law.

John Ude said, 'Come, come, dears, don't lose your temper. She'll get over it. Nathalie, what do you carry?' And the whole thing was over.

Much later Cassie, her face grey in the grey dusk, woke me accidentally. She's hunting in the first-aid kit, her face drawn.

She says, 'Oh, *you*! Go back to sleep.'

I said, 'What's the matter?'

'Migraine,' she said. 'I lost my pills. But this stuff is no good.' (The last with a little wail; I judged it hadn't come on yet, maybe just the flashes of light or whatever it is she gets first.) I said, 'Hold on,' and fished something out of my belt. Should help.

'So what's that, cyanide?' she whispered, closing her eyes as if to concentrate. It must be starting.

'No,' I said. 'It's like your pills. Better than that all-purpose pain-killer nonsense, anyway. Go on.' I held them out in my palm.

'Bet it's poison,' she said, but she took it. I saw her feel her way to the water dispenser over the uneven ground, cup a little water in her hand, and throw her head back. She came back and lay down on the mattress, out under the nothing sky. Still clear. Still no stars. One keeps getting the oddest feeling that it must be cloudy, though we've only seen morning fog. The temperature doesn't go down much at night. There's too much light, though; it's like living naked. Sometimes this place looks like a stage-set or a little alleyway or back yard of somebody's familiar country home; only in the true dark does it become real.

(Like the Australian outback, as I told them in my great lecture, which looks like New Jersey and can kill you in two hours.)

She said, 'What happens now, I blow up?' She cocked an eyebrow at me.

'No,' I said, smiling (I couldn't help it). 'The pain stops, and if it doesn't you won't care; it's got a euphoric in it, too.'

'Ooh, I'm gonna get high,' she said. 'Jollies . . . ' (Taking hold already?) 'Say, hon, how come you carry all that stuff?'

I explained: it's better than money. And you never know.

'All *you'd* need is a jack-knife,' she said, 'if you feel like cutting your throat, which is a goddamn cowardly thing to do, if you don't mind my saying so.'

'Good night,' I said, and turned over. I wasn't facing her any more.

'Hey!' (comes the voice at my back). 'You really want to kill yourself? You like getting hurt?'

'Yes, I want to do it before I get didded,' I said. 'And no. No follows from yes.'

She chuckled sleepily. 'Sorry I hit you. Forgive me, huh? What's that you said about the whozis and the old guy?'

(The old guy preached a sermon in his shroud a week before his death. The whozis were the Northmen; folks used to say Deliver us from fire, plague, the fury of the Northmen, *and sudden death*. Those crazy people who took months to die. They had things to think about.)

'Go to sleep,' I said. 'Dream about your migraines.'

And all the things. Such a beautiful world, really. But no music, no friends. If Earth had been hit by plague, by fire, by war, by radiation, sterility, a thousand things, you name it, I'd still stand by her; I love her; I would fight every inch of the way there because my whole life is knit to her. And she'd need mourners. To die on a dying Earth — I'd live, if only to weep.

But this stranger has never seen us before. She says: Hey, what are you funny little things? We are (O listeners, note) one quarter the height of the trees, we are hairless, give birth to our young alive, are bipedal with two manipulating limbs, have binocular vision, we regulate our internal temperatures by the slow oxidation of various compounds (food), and we live no more than a century at the very, very most (at least it feels that way, as the joke goes) and we are caught rather nastily, very badly, and sometimes even comically, between different aspirations. That is the fault of the cerebral cortex. (People are turning over, sighing, mumbling in their sleep, as the light slowly grows.)

Note: *ars moriendi* is Latin. It is a lost skill. It is ridiculed and is practiced by few.

It is very, very important.

It is the art of dying.

★

Day three. Alan-Bobby found a medallion among my personal effects (he was sorting everyone's; somehow they haven't gone looking for water yet), and being a nice, obedient little boy, took it to Victor Graham, who took it to John Ude.

'What is it?' said they (in chorus, as I imagine).

He told them. He came over to me (I was making a deck of playing cards from Mrs Graham's collection of antique post cards by first trying to peel the backs off) and swung the medallion at me, just far enough away so I couldn't grab it. Picture one early Christian, sitting cross-legged on the ground with lap covered by bedsheets, in case the cards didn't work out, and one professor – but not John Donne – who has decided to Tease.

'Now we know!' said John Ude, looking much less cosmopolitan than before.

'That? That's not mine,' I said. (When in doubt, deny.)

'Come! Who cares?' he said. (Alan and Victor have gone back to whatever they were doing; I'm sure he asked them to leave 'so I can get her to talk' or something.) 'Be anything you like. Only it explains what happened yesterday, and if I explain to everyone else, they might feel a little better about you.'

'You mean they'll dismiss me as a nut,' I said. 'All right, it's mine.' He held it out to me, but I really have no particular use for the thing, and the metal chain might be useful to someone else. I said:

'Look, it's only a symbol. You know, the quartered circle, symbol of Earth and all that. Keep it. Use the chain.'

'Don't you want it?'

'No. It's only a piece of jewelry.'

'Then you're not . . . ?'

'I am. But I don't use the Tarot, believe in the I Ching, tell fortunes, make sacrifices, have rituals, believe in the Bible – not literally, anyway – the Tao Te Ching, or anything else. So keep it.'

'An apostate!' he said.

'Oh, don't be silly.' And I went on trying my fingernails on the post cards. Don't see why she can't collect holovision cubes like everyone else. Have to use sheets, anyway. I said, 'Do you know how to play poker?'

But he had levered himself down on the grass next to me. No poison ivy so far. I said:

'Well, when are you guys going to find water?'

'A Trembler,' he said. 'My God, a Trembler in our very midst.' I shut my eyes.

'The Quakers,' I said, 'called themselves the Society of Friends. They were called Quakers because some fool heard John Fox say he quaked in the presence of his God. Actually I like to think of myself as a temblor. Never mind.'

'But you tremble.'

'Oh, all the time.'

'Do you believe in God?'

'No.'

'But you believe in something?'

'Everywhere. Always. See Lao-tse: Tao is in the excrement, in the broken tile. Cleave the rock and there am I. Now go away.'

'But tell me,' he said, professional passion rising, 'what does your church –'

'No church.'

'Well, what do you say about – about, say, sex?'

'Nothing.'

Mrs Graham, within earshot, having found that the tool chest was water-tight by filling it with water and having Lori take a bath in it, along with most of our clothes, caught guess-what-word. She wiped her hands free of suds and strolled over.

'May I join you?'

'I'm asking,' said John Donne, 'what the Tremblers have to say about sex.'

'Oh, that,' said Mrs Graham, looking knowing. It was real knowledge, too; you'd think Cassie, with her silver nipples, was the expert, but I think Cassie's frigid. She only sells it. Mrs G has been a buyer, and buyers do what buyers want.

'Well, what do they say?' says Valeria.

'Nothing,' I said. 'Look, Mrs Graham, I think you'd better keep your post cards to entertain your great-grandchildren. My fingers hurt and besides, there's no reason to sacrifice them; they're entertaining. I'll cut up a sheet.'

'And about —'

'Look, John,' I said, 'we are not a church, only an attitude. Our principal subjects are work and mortality, not fucking. On those two I could tell you a lot but you heard it all yesterday and didn't like it. So why don't you get Nathalie to activate the broomstick and let her go look for water on it? It's a hell of a lot faster than walking.'

'No, one of us will have to go,' said he, 'unless Mrs Graham can drive . . . ?'

'You see,' he went on, 'Nathalie's life and yours and Lori's and Cassie's are too valuable to put in danger. You are childbearers. What does your religion say about that?'

'Genetic drift —' I said.

'Civilization must be preserved,' says he.

'Civilization's doing fine,' I said. 'We just don't happen to be where it is.'

'Your church —'

'My religion,' said I, rising from my cross-legged position without uncrossing my legs (which rather surprised him, but it's easy for short people), 'says a lot about power. Bad things! It says thou owest God a death. It says that the first thing a sane civilization does with cryogenic corpses is to pull the plug on those damned popsicles, and if you want to live forever you are dreadfully dangerous because you're not living now. It says that you must die, because otherwise how can you be saved? It says that without meaningful work you might as well be dead. It also says death hurts. And it says if you try to be strong and perfect and good and powerful, you're a damned fool and liar and the truth is not in you. So don't try my patience. It also says God is in you and you are in God, as the fish is in the sea and the sea is in the fish. Saint Theresa. It *also* says —'

19

'You're a remarkably eclectic bunch,' said John Ude, laughing. 'Do you believe all this stolen theology?'

'Why not?' I said. 'I stole it myself.'

'Anyway, that's your field,' I added. He laughed. Indulgently.

'I'll spread the word,' he said. He walked off – even a twenty-five-hour day ends eventually – and happened to pass by Lori in the tool chest, who crossed her arms over herself with great rapidity and looked sheer murder at him. Odd morés: body paint's OK but bathing is private. Surrounded by clothes, too, all colors, bobbing about in the water. Barely room enough for the lot of them, her knees under her chin.

Mrs Graham said, 'Do you believe in life after death?'

'No,' I said.

'Oh. And when was the last time you slept with anyone?' I stared at her. She did not even look much interested.

I shrugged. 'Years ago. Dunno. A long time.'

'And *you're* living in the present?' she said, raising her eyebrows. 'Well!' Valeria Victrix. My God, yes, she must have been. In her own element.

'There's other things,' I said.

'Like – ?'

'Oh look, Mrs G –'

'Don't call me Mrs Gee,' she said. 'It's tasteless, don't you think? Call me Valeria. And tell me what all those wonderful other things are, besides sex. And money. Because you can turn money into anything, you know.'

Ah. I'm at the bottom of the pecking order now. Well, there are worse places, like the top. Inciting to riot. Destroying government property. (Symbolic?) I got arrested and was in jail overnight but I certainly wasn't at the center of it. No doubt one of those thirty-year cycles of rebellion Our Man John writes about. And as if they had no connection with physical fact. At the bottom you can hide effectively. I said:

'I was a Communist. I was in the 'twenties riots. Not very important, mind you, but it seemed to be going somewhere.'

'Just after hydrogen fusion,' said she. 'Which took the steam out of your sails, didn't it? And made me rich. So you're a Communist. Good Heavens! And a Trembler, too? I thought they didn't go together.'

'They do,' I said. 'Very well. And I'd prefer it if you called me what we call ourselves: Nobodies — I'm Nobody, who are you? Are you Nobody, too? How nice. Which is no bar to being a Communist. Which I was.'

'You're not one any longer?' she said.

'Mrs Gee,' I said, 'none of us is anything any longer.'

'Frigid little woman,' she said, stepping back. I said, 'Oh, call me a salad, why don't you, that makes as much sense. And think of what I could call you.'

'Motherrrr!' (Lori) She's tired of intimacies with everybody's washing.

'Oh, Valeria,' I went on, 'the heart is deceitful and desperately wicked, who can know it?' (She doesn't recognize, thinks I'm crazy.) I said, more prosaically, 'If you bother me again, I'll poison Lori's mind against you.'

She got up slowly, saying, 'At least I remember that I had something,' and went to pull Lori out of the washtub. A sensible woman, really, but she's going to learn she has no money here. I yelled, 'Hey, don't bug Victor, he's bigger'n you!'

'Victor Graham is *my father*,' cried Lori, reaching a glass for the cold-water dispenser, to rinse herself. 'Agh!' she cried. She shouted at me, 'My father would never do anything wrong!'

'Absolutely, love!' I shouted back. That child will grow up in a perfect mess of illusions.

Did grow up.

George Fox went to jail because he could not forbear rushing into Anglican services and denouncing their priesthood as mummery; he said the great bell struck upon his heart. I was not there, of course; read it in a book. The scores of thousands of books and musical compositions that are preserved in nitrogen at the British Museum in London. Prisoners and political exiles write books.

Would you write a book if you were alone on a desert island? Would you scratch in the sand?

Note: We communicate by organs that produce vibrations in the air (gaseous medium). We hear, roughly, sounds from 14 to 8,000 cycles per second. 'Sound' is a series of concentric rings made of the rarefaction and compression of air, water, or some other medium. We can't exist completely submerged in water (this may come as a shock to you), as the oxygen we use in our metabolisms comes out of the air. We're not equipped the other way. We draw air into ourselves and push it out. We are extremely fragile, propaganda to the contrary. 'Speaking' comes from a different place than 'breathing.' You must understand this. Those marks, '–', indicate speech. Communication. You must listen. You must understand that the patriarchy is coming back, has returned (in fact) in two days. By no design. You must understand that I have no music, no books, no friends, no love. No civilization without industrialization! I'm very much afraid of death. But I must. I must. I must.

Deliver me from the body of this. This body. This damned life.

Day four. Nathalie finally went off on the broomstick because nobody knew how to operate it but her and me. I was not allowed, naturally. I relented and showed Alan-Bobby how to use the axe without cutting off his feet. He took it away from me. He was cutting wood and so was Mr Graham, with the little hand hatchet; when they managed to collect some branches, they lit them to see if they could make a fire. Bravo! It burned. And the smoke gave Lori a violent allergic reaction; she ran away clawing at her throat, crying, viciously rotating her fingers in her ears, and making the tongue motions of someone trying (ineffectually) to scratch her soft palate. Perfect for the long winter evenings. So they put the fire out.

Mrs Graham played gin with Mr Graham, with the cards I'd made from bed linen; she kept beating him.

Then she played gin with John Ude and kept beating him.

He said he wished to walk about, still being gracious; Mrs G tried to get Mr G back into playing. He said, 'I don't wish to.'

'But I want to, dear,' said Valeria quietly. (A simple, domestic request, repeated many times; Valeria in blue and gold, the nail of her left little finger a gold sheath, inches long, Victor in blue, the evening game, Mrs Graham saying, 'Get me a drink, dear,' and Victor eager and compliant. Now I know.)

Victor got up and went to talk to Alan-Bobby, who chuckled and nodded; then they got *really serious*, about drainage ditches or log cabins, or burning other wood, for Victor would not hurt his daughter, that I do know, not for the world.

Something odd about Valeria's face. See, Victrix?

She said, 'Lori, I'm afraid your silly father has given you hives.'

'Daddy isn't silly,' (says oblivious young Graham, cleaning her toenails with a complicated spiral device that was apparently part of her personal baggage) 'and I don't think you should ask him to play cards if he doesn't want to. You can be awfully mean, Mother.'

I walked over to – no, I thought of walking over –

She came over to me. 'Do you play gin?' I shook my head.

'You see how they treat me,' and she tossed back that old-young face, that surgically lifted neck, with hair that has begun to come in gray at the roots. It's a beautiful gesture and I myself would be quite content simply to admire it no matter the age of the one who makes it, but I don't think the men will feel the same way.

'Oh, they're bored,' I said. 'It's nothing. Cultural reversion. We're in the late nineteenth century is all. Do you want to bet how far back we'll be next week? Five to ten it'll be the eighth A D.'

'You're crazy,' said Mrs Graham, not without affection, and went into the bungalow to make friends with Cassie.

I hid the crucial parts of my pharmacopoeia under a rock, in the tin box I will use for the vocoder, eventually. I thought of telling them I'm a vegetarian, just to make them discount even more of what I do (and they would!) but I couldn't do it with a straight face.

An endless afternoon.

John Ude: 'You play Go? Chess?' I said No, dunno why, never learned.

Lori remarked that she didn't see what was wrong with the Australian outback because she'd been there, in the special hotel, and it was very, very nice.

I donate my mini-sewing-kit to the communal possessions heap.

Finally, after Cassie had walked six ways around a bedsheet, deciding how to cut it up and sew it for herself, after everyone had memorized the kind of tree whose burning had made Lori sick ('This is very important' said her father), after Lori said 'Oh, I am like to die of tedium' only a dozen times, before we all went mad –

Nathalie returned on the broomstick, covered with dust. There's running water not far from here, *that* way (she gestures) which rises (she says) in a spring some two hundred kilometers to the North, in hilly country, and passes us only a couple of km away.

'Did you have to go all that way?' says Alan-Bobby, in grave complaint. 'We've been just waiting around.'

She throws over her shoulder, 'Of course I had to,' and sponging off the mask near the water tank, starts drawing on one of my playing cards where the stream is, where we are, and in which direction everything is. 'North' is provincial. She means Polewards. At this time of year you can't tell East or West from the sun; though perhaps the sunset (a little to the right) and the sunrise (a little to the left) could tell us if we are facing North or South. Arbitrary. I study it very carefully.

'Will you just stop that!' cries Nathalie furiously, for Alan is taking a bath in the tool chest, a real bath (insofar as he can fit in) and singing lustily, though nothing recognizable. He's tune-deaf. Nathalie shouts, 'Goddamn it, you're wasting water!'

'But we've got water,' says he, bewildered. 'You just said so.'

'We've got the raw material for the distiller,' she said. 'That's all. We haven't even measured the flow yet. Now get out of there!'

He does, tipping the soapy water on to the ground, where it might make the grass wither or blow up (but it doesn't) and prepares to fill the tool box again.

'You . . . !' says Nathalie, white. 'You imbecile!'

'I don't think,' says Alan, slowly, like a man to whom a new idea has just occurred, 'that you ought to talk to me like that.'

'We could've put that back through the distiller!' (Which is what we've been doing with our chemical toilet.)

'I think you are much too bossy,' says Alan, sponging himself off with a few inches of cold water. He's looking at the ground and something's happening in his head. John Ude has backed off, smiling nervously. Victor's frowning.

Nobody likes her, not Cassie, not Mrs Gee, not her husband, certainly. Lori and I don't count.

Dried off and in his shorts, Alan advances up to dirty, dust-streaked Nathalie, who has always been Top. He looks sly.

'Say, how come you're boss?' he says.

'Brains,' she says. 'How come you're such a damn fool?'

'I could take you over my knee and spank you,' he says.

Nobody is interfering.

'Idiot,' says she. Clearly, in government training schools people don't do these things.

She turns her back on him, superbly.

'Look, nobody else can fly that thing,' I say, very quickly. 'And since you won't let me because you don't trust me, you'd better –'

'Turn around,' he says.

She props the broomstick against a tree, stripping off her shirt and beating the dust out of it.

'Turn around, you bitch!' he says.

Surprised, she does. Not even afraid. Only surprised.

And Alan-Bobby, who could probably uproot a tree, with those shoulders and arms and that neck, and the little face in between looking peculiarly lost – but very angry now – socks her right in the jaw, knocking her down.

He's red. He says, 'Maybe now you'll treat other people with respect. Now that you know there's other people in the world.'

She whispers, sprawled on the ground, white as one of my playing cards, 'You bloody, blazing, impossible ass –'

He hits her powerfully on the side of the face, snapping her head about.

'That's enough,' says Victor, he and John Ude, by some mysterious calculus, speaking almost at the same moment, and each coming forward to hold one arm of this baby colossus. Enough for what? Alan looks happy. I mean it: not triumphant, not overbearing, simply happy. He glows. The twenty-first century can't have been kind to this enormous fellow, and now he's discovering other interesting things to do: chopping down trees, lifting rock with his bare hands, fighting, knocking down women. Too bad he's so young; Victor Graham now, there's a hypertensive if I ever saw one; once his medication runs out, we might do a job like the old Jewish story: the Rabbi and the Count both tied to chairs, alone in the Count's cellar for a whole night, and in the morning the Rabbi serene and fresh and the Count a dead man. Apoplexy.

But Alan's useful.

Any day now he'll discover Protecting Women. I hope.

Valeria Victrix got the first-aid kit, and she and I anointed and bandaged Nathalie, who was still shaking – more from anger than from shock. Cassie pushed us aside, claiming she could do it better. She was right.

I said, 'Nathalie, I thought a government trainee would know –'

'I will, I will,' she said.

'My God, why didn't you duck?' I said. 'Or just drop under his punch? Or give him a good knee-over when you were on your back? Or stick your fingers in his eyes?'

Well, he had surprised her. Cassie thought any woman who even got into such a position was a fool to begin with. 'Just tell him Lori is watching,' she said. 'And cry a lot. You're both cuckoo.'

I said, 'Look here, Nathalie, just how much training have you really had?'

Silence.

Of course. She was going to it, not coming *from* it.

I said quickly, 'Never mind. Don't speak; your mouth is puffing up.'

Sitting, holding rags soaked in cold water to her face. Streaked with dirt. John, Victor, and Alan making ecstatic plans how to move everything nearer the stream. We go to bed when the sun reaches a certain clump of trees; there's hours of daylight yet to go and nobody can tell if the day is getting shorter or longer. It remains warm, too light, but better that than that dreadful, empty, black sky.

You see the rewards of being Nobody.

The penalty: everybody comes to me for advice. Because my public word would not be trusted, I can be told anything privately. Alan whispers:

'Hey, wake up. Please?'

Dusk all around us. Scarlatti in my head. I said, 'What?'

'Are you awake?' he whispered. I mumbled something and opened my eyes. Dusk or dawn, everybody's mattresses scattered all over the ground, farther apart than last night. I've got to get away from these insane people. Alan is lying by my mattress on the damp ground, his woeful face propped in his hands. He says, in a low voice so as not to waken anyone:

'Do you think what I did was really so bad?'

'Yes,' I said. 'Absolutely.'

'Lori chewed me out something awful,' he said. 'So did Mrs Graham. And Cassie won't speak to me.'

I sat up. I said, 'I bet Ude gave you a lecture on civilization and Vic said you'd have him to reckon with if you tried it again.'

'How'd you know!'

'Oh, just guessing,' I said.

'Well, do you think it was so bad?' Looking anxious.

'Yes. Now let me sleep. Git.'

'Hell, you sound just like Nathalie! I'll tell you, maybe it wasn't right, but I bet it taught her something!'

'What did it teach her?' I said. 'Never to approach you without a broken bottle in her hand? Now Lori thinks you're real sweet. And Vic Graham knows that some day you're going to pull something like that on him. It taught us all to love and trust you. Right?'

He sat back on his heels. He said sulkily, 'I could do it to you, too, you know.'

I said, 'Really, Victor? Sorry – slip of the tongue,' and was on my feet, holding straight out in that treacherous light the screwdriver I had abstracted from the tool chest on day one.

You surely don't think I'm fool enough to walk about without a weapon, do you?

He reached for it, and I gave his hand a good slash. He withdrew it, extremely astonished.

'Oh, go away,' I said. 'I haven't the slightest intention of hurting you and you don't have the slightest intention of really hurting me. You're just showing off. You're a good, big, strong, decent, beautiful man, and you can pride yourself on that all you like. But don't forget; even though she's exasperating, *Nathalie is smart* and if you start throwing your weight around nobody else will like you and she'll take advantage of that. Remember: you're not stronger than all of us put together. Besides, Lori's stuck on you.'

He lit up. 'Yeah!'

'So go to sleep now, huh?'

He said, 'How old do you think Lori would have to be before she can have babies?'

'Sixteen,' I said (guessing). 'Now go to sleep.'

Day five: we'll move everything nearer the river, like lemmings. Nathalie will start turning bruise-blue in the face. Alan will creep about like a wounded pup, ostracized by all, scorned by Lori Graham, the worst burdens loaden on his back, meke as the knyght that suffereth for his ladye's sake.

Which won't last.

Day five: we worked eighteen hours, slept, worked again. Alan has reverted to the intensely polite, self-suppressing youth everybody knew and loathed. My feet hurt. I tried to explain about orthopedic malfunctions and was told I was malingering. Then my ankles swelled out most satisfactorily in the evening, looking distressingly like small cantaloupes, and everyone was most apologetic. I said No, no, I had to carry my share. Then my ankles got even more so. Cassie washed them, the great nurse, sexpot, earth-mother. We went to bed. She says: 'Sssst!'

Me: What?

She: You ever had an orgasm?

Me: Can't remember.

She: Liar. I mean during fucking. I never did. Women are all liars about it, like Vicki Graham. She just pretends, to show off, you know.

(Silence.)

She: Ever want babies?

Me: I dunno. Sort of. Not really.

She: I do.

(Silence.)

She: They don't let you, if you're poor. But here —

Me: I see. Well, good luck. How are you going to handle the men?

She just laughed. Then she said with perfect certainty, 'Those babies'll love me, not their daddies.' She nudged me. 'Hey, mad-head, Ude and Graham are going to take your pills away from you in the morning.'

'And who told them, you bloody traitor!' said I.

'Sssssh!' She looked around uneasily, then whispered, 'I did.'

She added, 'But I told you too, didn't I?'

Day six: I am set upon from behind, bound, and searched, protesting indignantly. They slit the lining of my jacket (Cassie: 'Oh, don't take on so; I'll sew it up again!'), violate my leather belt ('Hey, look, it's got pop-outs,' says Alan), and pinch my body-suit up and down (without me in it, of course). They collect all the psychedelics. I cry, very very hard. They free my hands so I can blow my nose and I whack Cassie, who looks startled. Then they let me put on my body-suit and Victor Graham stands very impressively in front of me, hands out: 'More.'

'Me?' I said. 'Me have anything more? I swear —'

Finally I unscrew my left shoe-heel and give them Cassie's

headache medicine. Then I unscrew my right shoe-heel and hand over a glass vial. Victor starts to crush the thing, and this part of the scene is genuine, believe me; I yelled 'Don't! Stop!'

Consternation.

I said, 'That's lethal. It's a nerve poison, works right through the skin. You don't have to drink it. Victor! Just put it down. No, it's not bio-degradable, so you can't put it in the chemical toilet. Just leave it in the sun for a while. That'll ruin it. *But don't let anybody touch it.*'

Victor confers with John Ude, both of them gingerly handling the vial. Ude nods. I've told the truth. (And I have. What I did not tell them was how many more I've got hidden back at the old site.) I started to cry harder, which isn't difficult because I'm thinking of how damned unfair it is that I shall never hear again my melancholy Dowland: *semper Dowland, semper dolens.* Ever Dowland, ever doleful. No tee-hee-hee-quoth-she for him. I noticed through my tears that Nathalie appears to have formed some kind of alliance with John Ude, her moral impressiveness having proved unequal to Alan's muscles. The two intellectuals. The two bureaucrats. Tee-hee-hee in the mattress. They don't want to set me free, but that is foolish, as I tell them at great length, and I cry a lot harder, and even rock back and forth, which is nine parts fury, until Cassie says, 'Oh stop it, hon, I'll fix your jacket. What were you going to do with those things, anyway? Kill yourself by an overdose?'

'No,' said I. 'I just feel humiliated.' She put her arm around me, which is enough to make you feel an awful bemmon. She then promised to fix my jacket.

I gave them back the screwdriver.

Oh, it went like a charm!

John Ude, still uncontrollably curious, says to me on the last trek back to the old place: 'Really, I cannot understand why you want to die.'

'Neither can I,' I said.

'Well, then?'

I said, 'John Donne, John-John-with-your-britches-on, John-Whittington-turn-again-lord-mayor-of-London-Town, we *are* dead.

We died the minute we crashed. Plague, toxic food, deficiency diseases, broken bones, infection, gangrene, cold, heat, and just plain starvation. I'm just a Trembler. My God, you're the ones who want to suffer: conquer and control, conquer and control, when you haven't even got stone spears. You're dead.'

'For dead people, we're acting pretty brisk,' says Ude, with The Smile. Haven't seen that for a while; Nathalie must've bucked him up quite a bit.

'It's one of the symptoms,' I said. 'Galvanism. Corpse jerking. Planning. Power. Inheritance. You know, survival. My genes shall conquer the world. That's death.'

'Hear you were quite big in that power and planning stuff about fifteen years back,' he says.

'Then you heard wrong. I walked out one day and gave it all up. Hideously ineffectual.'

'Still –'

'For everything there is a time and a season under Heaven; now you ought to know that.'

He keeps on smiling The Smile. No recognition.

I said, 'You're not a historian of ideas.'

'Clever,' says he. 'I wondered when you'd tumble to it. I was what you'd call a bureaucrat. That's why Nathalie and I get along. She says we think alike.'

'Sure, after yesterday,' said I. Ude halted.

'Don't push us,' he said. 'Don't you push us too much now.'

'Then leave me alone,' I said. 'Just leave me alone and I'll have no reason to push anybody, huh?'

But they won't be able to leave me alone. I know. Not because of the child-bearing, because of the disagreement. The disagreement is what matters.

How far will I push them? To where? All the way?

Day seven: as lunatics or lemmings will, we dragged our glass-and-plastic bungalow, the only dwelling with a heater this side of God-knows-what, two kilometers to the stream, the

31

travois being its own light-but-stubborn bottom. It took all day. Too tired to do anything else. Lying on the mattress outdoors, Nathalie sketching in the dirt the plans of sanitary latrines (downstream). Quickly goes in and washes and disinfects her hands. No one has yet deliberately ingested one morsel of anything in this place; still we must have been breathing in and swallowing a good deal, and no one's dead yet. We live on the freeze-dried. How to test it out? A fruitless (sorry) question.

They asked me to sing. My memory was stuck on Dowland; I thought of 'Flow, My Tears,' 'In Darkness Let Me Dwell,' 'A Heart That's Broken' — well! This is not good public relations. 'Come All Ye Sons of Art'? Nothing with polyphony. Finally I sang 'Sweet Kate' with all the tee-hee-hee. Taught Cassie, who has a good natural voice, to come in on it, and added a few nasty Renaissance songs about jealousy (dreadful people), 'Farewell, Unkind,' and finished with a sudden burst of remembrance, swooping in great fake arcs, those posh-velveteen melodies:

> Blue desert
> And you and I . . .

(Where on earth did I learn 'The Desert Song'?)
Lori sang Gilbert and Sullivan and forgot the middles.

'Oh, you *can* sing!' cried Alan, in a burst of admiration (at me, not at Lori; the mystic maiden can, of course, do anything).

Schubert! Of course. I said, 'More tomorrow.' But can I do the eleven-note jumps upward on an o-umlaut? Never. Ah! Sea songs and folk songs.

(Did I learn them in high school?)
Good night, court jester.

Day eight: the great womb robbery. The day started out well enough, with me limping so badly (at least I tried to) that I was excused work by John Ude, told, 'oh, that's too bad,' by several others, and ended up playing cards with Lori (I mean the bedsheet cards). For some reason nobody mentions she's never expected to do any work, God knows why. She kept beating me at Casino, while I rubbed my ankles.

'Are those orthopedic shoes?'

I said uh huh.

She yelled excitedly, 'I've got the ten of diamonds!' and took in an eight of clubs and a two of hearts. (That's three points.) She looked at me sideways, then stuck her nose up in the air.

'So you want us to kill ourselves!' she said, with contempt.

I just made a face and threw up my hands.

'You think nobody'll find us?' she added, a little sharper.

'Oh, I was just talking,' I said. She was counting up her winnings so far. She said, frowning, 'You're a coward!' and put her cards down in a neat little pile, with a stone on top of it.

I said uh huh again.

'The one thing my Mummy and Daddy taught me when they got me from the crèche when I was seven,' she said, still sharply, 'was never to give up on anything. And never to be a coward.' Five years of money, that's five years of enforced childishness. She started shuffling the cards in a very slow method invented by herself: put them in piles of three each, with a pebble on top, then take one off the top of each pile, then subtract every fourth card and put them on the bottom. I can't figure it. Daddy had set up a kind of awning with four stakes chopped from a tree and one of the sheets; we were sitting under this and watching the others sweat at the foundation of the communal house, about fifty meters away from the water and several meters above it on a slight elevation. Nathalie had suggested some kind of wooden rockers under the house, like the type used in Colonial New England: good for winds, for shifting ground, and floods. I don't know what they think they're going to insulate it with — wood shavings, chopped by hand?

Lori started to deal the cards. You have to pick each of them up with both hands and hold it taut: otherwise it drapes and you can see the other side. Managing a handful of them isn't easy. I said:

'Shall I tell your fortune?'

'Huh?' said she.

'Do you know how to read palms?'

She shook her head. 'That's silly.' She stuck out her hand, then giggled and drew it back.

'All right,' she said, after a moment. 'Go ahead. But I know what you'll say!'

'Hmm,' I said, 'do you now, little miss.' That struck her as excruciating: me, the gypsy. She put on an expression very like her mother's only far more exaggerated: eyes rolled up, corners of the mouth pulled down.

I said, 'You have an immensely long life-line.' (I cannot tell a life-line from a thumb.) 'Here,' I said at random. 'You will die sometime in your eighty-ninth year. You will be well-known. Even famous. Extraordinary!'

'Known to how many?' said Lori quickly.

'Millions,' I said (acting out vast surprise). 'Your life-line is interrupted here by . . . by relative isolation for a period of years . . . not many years, perhaps eight or nine. And then there's a great blossoming of renown, almost as great as what I see at the end of your life.'

'Well, obviously we're going to be saved,' she said pedantically.

'So it would seem. Here' (I think I was somewhere in the middle of her palm) 'is the line which indicates either children or good work, fruitful work. It branches four – five – no, many more times. But I don't know if that means children or work.'

'Work,' she said promptly. 'I'm a musician.'

'Oh,' I said.

'Yes,' (and she nodded); 'I'm a composer.'

'Are you? Think of that!'

'Well, I will be,' she said. Then she added, 'That's the same thing. But I'll tell you a secret –' (she all but whispered this, leaning over the piles of cards) '*I don't like commercial music.*'

'Oh,' I said. What hearts did I wring when I was a child? Just a biological device, Nature keeping us old ones in the service of the young.

34

She said, frowning, 'You look funny.'

Then she added, without the slightest transition, 'I like serial music. You know, the late-twentieth-century stuff where it goes deedle deedle deedle deedle deedle deedle deedle deedle for half an hour and then it goes doodle just once, and you could die with excitement.'

'Uh huh,' I said.

'I've written one – well, half of one – composition.' She stuck out her hand. 'Go on.'

I said, 'You know, Lori, what I think your fortune means is that you will not only be famous for music, but also for having been rescued here. They'll probably call the place after you. They do things like that, you know.'

'Of course,' she said. 'And everybody gets rescued. As my father was trying to tell you.'

'John Ude was trying to tell me, I believe,' I said.

'*My father!*' She stuck out her hand. 'Go on.'

'It's a musician's hand,' I said shamelessly, 'that's true. And the rest . . . well, I can't see much out of the ordinary except riches, of course . . . you know that . . . I think you will write a book about your experiences – *here*' (pointing) 'but of course I can't tell whether that's a book or music. The wealth line increases at that point. And marriage –'

'I'll *never* get married.'

'Yes, there's hardly anything. Though your love line is quite another thing. But who, of course, or even what, I can't tell.'

'Artistic passion?' said she.

'Mm hm. And the rest . . . well, it doesn't tell us anything we don't know. Sensitive. Intellectual. But animal vitality, mustn't forget that. That's about it.'

'Oh,' she said. She was disappointed.

'It changes,' I said, 'almost day to day. Most people don't know that. Small changes, of course, nothing big. But that's all I can see today.'

'You'll do it again in a week,' said Lori decisively, beginning to deal her cards. It did not seem to occur to her that she was giving me orders. I pictured her giving orders to Alan-Bobby.

No.

She dealt the cards, a very finicky young woman, concentrating deeply.

Suddenly she said, 'Are you really a coward?'

'No,' I said.

'Yes you are,' she said. 'Pick up your cards. If you teach me to read palms, I'll read *your* palm. That'll tell us.'

She won the next game, too.

We were well into our third and Lori was singing something from Gilbert and Sullivan about not telling him, her, or it, because etiquette didn't permit, and not even hinting, whispering, or pointing it out – yes, very apposite – and I was bored – when Alan shouted 'Over here, everyone!' because he had the big voice. They had been slacking work for some time, with a lot of talk between Nathalie, the ex-professor, and Victor. (One to dig, two to chop, and two to carry either logs or dirt in the tool chest: Nathalie, Alan, Valeria – with the hand hatchet – Victor, Ude.) Symptoms of a conference.

'Bring your tent!' shouted Alan conscientiously.

So we did – rather, I did; Lori wouldn't touch it for fear that she might break out in hives. I told her while I was uprooting it (and not entirely out of compassion; she could be a real whiner when she chose) that she'd live to be eighty, name all the plants in the region, lose her allergies as she grew up, and end up writing the first book about Lori's Planet.

The court. Under another jury-rigged tent. After this my memories get a little muddled. Disturbance: ripples in a pond. I smiled mechanically. Won't be thought a good, reliable witness –

(*By whom?*)

reliable witness.

Victor's very big. *Very* polite. So you can't get at him, perhaps. Valeria was off to one side, with Cassie. Victrix patted the ground next to her invitingly and Lori stared carefully in another direction. Alan, awed, with his mouth open; John Ude peculiarly cool; and Nathalie grimly watching the ground.

Mister-not-Professor Ude said, 'I call this meeting to order.'

Oh. Oh my. Important.

'You're chairman?' I said. 'Well! Who made you chairman?'

Nathalie: 'I did.'

That is, they both did. Things are going to be very interesting.

Victor: 'That's a valid objection. I suggest we begin by selecting a chair.'

Silence. Then Nathalie said wearily, 'I nominate' – Guess Who? – well, he was nominated, seconded, and voted in. Almost unanimously.

John Ude: 'Do you have any more objections?'

Me: 'No.'

(Almost unanimously means me and Lori, Lori because she wanted her father to be, and I abstained.)

'We have to talk about something very important,' said Ude. 'I mean having children.'

Hand up, me. He recognized me – does this sound as crazy to you as it does to me? – and I said, 'Priorities backwards. First we have to poison Lori.'

'Huh?' she said; 'you're crazy.'

'Mr Chairman,' I said, 'point of order. Is it necessary for us to pretend that we've never met before?'

He smiled. Oh, the universes tremble when John Ude smiles! He said, 'I suppose we can afford to be somewhat more informal. In fact, I think it will be a very good thing. Please go ahead.'

I said, 'I'm only trying to suggest that before we start any babies, we'd better start finding out what we can eat around here.'

(Lori, sotto voce, with a dig in the ribs, 'Why'd you say poison?')

Cassie said, 'Sure, why the baby?'

'I was joking,' I said. 'I meant she's allergic to so many things. She should be the last person to eat anything.'

Nathalie: 'Will you volunteer to be the first?'

'No,' I said. 'Will you?'

Nathalie got up, very angry. 'We have food and water for five months and three weeks! Perhaps you'd like the rest of us to eat grass and leave it all to you?'

'I waive it,' I said. 'I leave it alone. Give me the broomstick and I'll go up to the head of the stream and drink the water without the purifier. If I start hurting, I'll kill myself.'

'This is no time for joking.' (John Ude)

I said, 'I'm not joking. It's a genuine offer.'

Silence.

'About the children,' said Ude. 'Mister Graham, as the oldest of us, has offered to donate his genetic material first.'

Cassie giggled.

Nathalie glared at her. But Nathalie also sat down.

(Was Victor on a special diet, on the ship?)

I got up and ambled toward the stream. By all that's alive, a melodramatic 'Stop!' and then 'Stop her!' from John Ude, and here was Alan-Bobby running ahead of me, like some crazy postman with a Special Delivery (excuse me) and turning sheepishly to stand in front, his arms stretched out.

'All right,' I said, 'all right, I can go taste the river when you're asleep, can't I?' and I headed back toward the improvised council tent, feeling in my palm the pellet-gun. Reflex. Not here, not now. Back in the sleeve of the jacket you go.

How'd it get there?

Oh, I forgot to tell you . . .

Between yesterday and today, when everyone was asleep, I went back to the old site and dug everything up. Including my pharmacopoeia. Left them lying on the ground with dreams of 'The Desert Song' ringing in their ears. (I had mist-spray hypnotics in my underwear. I'm not *that* quiet.) I tiptoed off, anyway, felling Alan-Bobby as he sat up, probably talking in his sleep, with a swift squish to the nostrils and, very daring, went off on the trudge to the old camp, where it took me forever to pry up that rock. I left in the dusk; I returned at the end of the dark: the sky ragged where the sun rises and sets, one patch of cloud red, red as blood, red as fury. I gave them each a last spray as I came, too. Except Lori. (She might be allergic.) She was wiggling and muttering uncomfortably to herself. Watched her face slowly settle itself and become clarified as the light grew and grew. Without getting anywhere – I mean the light – for hours and hours more.

'Hey, you better go back,' says Alan.

'Oh.' I sigh. 'Okay.' And go back, helpless.

Now I'm going to be first. I said, 'Well, you'll have to wait until I'm off the pills. And then it sometimes takes a few months to restore fertility. And we *don't* want septuplets, so that's another couple of months.'

'You're not taking any pills,' said Nathalie.

'Because you've never seen me do it? Whew!' said I. (That last's a whistle.)

'What are you taking?' said Ude.

I made up a name.

'Then you don't,' (he said, blinking slightly but looking steadily at me the while) 'have to worry about multiple births. There haven't been any on that since '07. I don't see why you and Victor can't start now, if you like.'

Victor said politely that he certainly wouldn't mind as long as I wouldn't mind.

I said I would mind.

'Why?' said Nathalie.

'Personal preference,' said I.

'It's her religion!' said Cassie, a little indignantly. 'You should respect a person's religion, you know.'

'She's probably *left-handed*.' This is Mrs Graham, spitefully. Cassie obviously wasn't sure what 'left-handed' meant; she leaned towards Mrs Graham, who whispered to her.

Cassie colored to the roots of her hair – and her neckline (a sheet).

'In a month, if you don't mind,' I said to Victor, with a sort of little bow. 'When it'll do most good.' Now he can't have liked that. But he looked unmoved and nodded his head. Polite. Cairn. Great, handsome, hollow monument of a man. Perhaps he's run out of something. Perhaps he's going to be ill. Hypertensive or cardiac, I can almost smell it. Or some other fatality hanging in the air and nobody wants to talk about it in front of the daughter. Get him before he dies.

'Before that month, then,' said John Ude, grinning in my direction, 'Nathalie has suggested herself, and afterwards the other lady, Cassie. The – uh – persons involved can certainly find privacy almost anywhere, I suppose. Anyway, it's none of our business.'

Cassie, who was folding the hem of her improvised dress under and over with her fingers, again and again, said:

'I'm going to be called by my full name. I don't like Cassie. That's only a professional name.'

'Of course,' said John Ude.

'Tell us,' said Victor.

Alan looked blankly receptive.

'My name is Cassandra,' said Cassie.

Nobody caught it. Lori said, 'That's a nice name,' (possibly to annoy her mother). I inhaled when I should've swallowed and for thirty seconds there until I stopped coughing John Ude was very tender and careful with his walking womb.

'Cassandra's always wanted children,' he said pleasantly to me when I could breathe again. Nathalie was behind him, looking over his shoulder.

I tried to call him a son-of-a-prick and only croaked.

'Yes?' he said, very alert – but he always seems alert; it's part of the window-dressing.

'Listen,' I whispered, just managing to speak. 'I'll go away. Take the broomstick and send it back, very slow, so you can catch it. Go upstream – downstream – doesn't matter – try the water. Take no food. Just leave me.'

'No!' said Nathalie.

'Why?' I coughed some more.

'If I've got to do it, you've got to do it,' said Nathalie.

'You . . . don't have to.' And I cleared my throat. At last.

'We'd better keep an eye on her,' said Nathalie to John Ude.

I think I put my head in my hands. Suppose they found my gun? My things? Wait long enough and it won't matter. Although I can always do it. Anyone can do it. Easy enough to kill if it doesn't matter about being found out. Then perhaps they'd kill me, and it would be over, and that's all right.

But I'm afraid of waiting too long. Eroding. Purpose all gone. Slipping into no-decision, no-purpose; hard enough as it is. God knows. I think everyone loves it here because their choices are all made for them; we were never very comfortable with our fate in our own hands, were we? Better to act on the modern religion: an incarnation of the immortal germplasm. Nostalgia for the mud. Simplicities.

I said, 'Cassandra!' and burst out laughing, coughing again.

'You're going mad,' said Nathalie, with a certain satisfaction and she and John Ude stepped backwards so they could talk, I suppose, about *keeping an eye on* me.

And nobody knows. Nobody knows anything about anything.

'Aren't you going to play cards with me?' said Lori, suddenly turning up with the cards in a sort of bag she'd made out of a scarf of her mother's. It was bright, bright blue. Royal blue.

'Sure,' I said. 'Why not?' And did.

Day nine. I took my turn digging and carrying. I was watched, always by someone. Nathalie and Victor disappeared dutifully over the hill while the rest of us snored (presumably).

Day ten. Watched. They overestimate their perseverance. At bedtime – the sun still circling around the same eternal altitude – Nathalie talked angrily about tying me to something for the night so's I wouldn't disappear. I told her not to be a fool; anything she could tie, I could untie.

People were embarrassed.

★

Day eleven. Idiot labor. A Long House none of us will ever live to enjoy. The food goes faster this way. A midday siesta under the tent, all of us huddled together in the shadow. But it merely gets hotter and hotter until sunset.

The sun is not changing its position, not fast enough to be timed, anyway. The weather stays the same. No rain, but the stream keeps up. By some eerie common consent Valeria has become the cook — good for nothing else, I suppose. That is, she prepares the packets of freeze-dried and pours stream water into the purifier. No one dead yet.

The idyllic desert island. Odd how that started out 'deserted' and ended up 'desert.' Hence the conventional sand and palm trees. No, 'desert' once meant only wild.

That it is.

Day twelve. Victor's ill. He sat all day under the tent, dozing and taking some sort of pills. Angina, I'll be bound.

More hauling, more digging on that idiot building.

Early evening (when the sun stands at four o'clock above a particular hill; we are in a little valley with a close horizon): Flop. Flop. Flop. Flop. Valeria and Victor have already flopped. Discarded pill-bottle on the ground. Lori's being kept away, mostly by Alan, sometimes by Nathalie, who says that she ought to work for a change.

(Lori stuck out her tongue. I giggled.)

Victor looked unconcerned at this invasion of his privacy: or not concerned, rather.

Lori said carelessly, 'Oh, Dad's had this before.' Valeria is paying no attention to him or to any of us; she's asleep. I have begun to be startled at anyone's coming up behind me, with a kind of shrinking at the presence of the rest of them, but Victor Graham is magnificently vacant; doesn't care that there are people around him.

We slept — we've gotten into the habit, it seems, of sleeping in stages: part in the middle of the 'afternoon,' then a siege before the dark, then a kind of premature wakefulness for a few hours until the twilight begins and depresses everybody. I seem to go to sleep faster than anyone, but I always wake a little earlier. Nervousness. I had my head by his knee.

Shocked awake.

Yawning. It wasn't anything, I thought.

Listening wakefully. Eyes open.

It's a little gasp from Victor Graham. He got up, holding (I think) his left arm with his right, for I saw him pass over me, and from that position on the ground, with my face down, it was like feeling a cloud go over you at an enormous height; I said he walked between us and over us, between two hills, Equator-wards.

He stopped to retch.

All I have to do is lie here and pretend to sleep.

He's walking off between the hills. Going to die alone, I suppose.

I got up carefully and picked my way to John Ude, put one hand over his mouth, and with the other, pinched him.

'Ssssh!' I jerked my head at Victor. You must say for the not-Professor that he takes things in quickly. We knew that neither of us must wake Lori and that she's the lightest sleeper of all because she hasn't worked.

'Where'd you put my stuff?' I whispered, off at the edge of the group.

His wits are wandering. He had to go back and wake Nathalie. And all the time, you know, it was burning a hole in my pocket, I mean my belt pop-out, the stuff he should be using; I was extraordinarily conscious of it sitting over my left hip-bone.

He came back with Nathalie, and we ran. Victor had sat down under one of the stumpy trees and was staring ahead of him. Nathalie, fingers shaking, spread out on the dirt the stuff they had confiscated from me and looked helplessly at Ude, who was beginning to frame a question, but I had it out and the string around his arm, the stuff into the vein. These are collapsible, permanent syringes, foldups like accordion pleating.

43

Nathalie said, 'Antisepsis —'

I said, 'Lie down, you fool,' to Victor, and he did. A little less livid, as the stuff got to him.

I said, 'It's a stimulant. Can you swallow?'

'No,' he said, still concentrating on the pain.

'You can,' I said, selecting from the pile, 'bite on this and breathe. It's a mind-bender; won't stop the pain, but it'll separate you from it. Takes the nastiness out of it.'

He did. Nathalie bent over, but I shooed her away. 'Do you want Lori?' I said.

'No.'

'Your wife?'

'Won't come.' He whispered, very carefully. The cyanotic grey was ebbing. I said:

'The stimulant is only temporary. I can give you more until we either run out of it or it wears you out, but I can't heal you. You may heal yourself if you lie very still.'

He said, 'Tell Lori —'

'What?' said Nathalie anxiously.

'Anything. Make it up.'

I said, 'Mister Graham has other things to do right now. We will tell Lori and Valeria that he thought of them, that his last words were of them, and that he loved them.'

The dying man laughed. 'Not – wife.'

'But I can tell Lori, can't I?' I said.

He nodded, just a bit.

'Victor loves his daughter and gives the planet to her. He's proud of her and knows she'll do well. Okay?'

'Yes!' His color was stealing back, almost magical, but it puts a worse burden on the great arteries crowning the heart. I said, 'I think you'd better go back and deal with the scene there. Both of you. When they wake up, you know; you can tell them whatever you like.'

'I?' said Nathalie. 'I'm supposed to be with him!' Victor's gaze was still so fixed that to get his attention you had to be right in front of

44

him. Nathalie put herself in front of me, directly in his line of vision; she had the anxiety lines of the brows furrowed together, in that very expressive field of musculature above and around the human eyes. The eyes themselves, you know, show almost nothing.

John Ude said, 'Perhaps I should stay —'

I said, 'Are you afraid of Lori?' and then to Victor, 'Who do you want to stay with you? Which of us?'

'You,' he said.

'Of course. She knows the drugs,' said John Ude with The Smile.

'You're not afraid,' he said, 'of me.'

Silence.

'Leave that and that and that,' I said, pointing. 'Now get cracking! You've work to do.'

'None of these is marked,' said Ude finally, gathering up half my things. (He thought he had it all.)

'I know,' I said. 'I also sell knowledge.' John Ude patted me on the shoulder: loathesome, loathesome! — said into my ear, 'Good of you.'

Victor said, with a smile, 'Are you sorry? You know . . .'

'I think I am,' I said. And almost was. Sorry for him, I mean. One thing dying people usually know, if they have any sense left, is what they want; and that is so rare in the human condition that it commands a certain kind of respect. Although I suppose they may know what they want only because there's so little left to choose from that the task's easy. It strips people down. And what I feel — or felt — about him, I don't know. An intense curiosity. Where he was going, where he came from, who he was. It's a world going out — though there are some worlds I know too well to care about, like Ude.

'I was poor,' he said. 'Didja know that?' I shook my head. Something of the old timbre back in his voice, still half a whisper. I could never find pulses in the wrist, so I put my fingertips on the great vein in his neck. He smiled. 'Feels nice,' he said. Then: 'I worked on myself. Made myself good-looking, you know:

45

clothes, accent, the works. Spent a lot on surgery; no whore could've done better.'

He grasped my hand, then let his arm fall but still kept holding on to my hand, I think out of fear, though he wasn't feeling any pain; couldn't have talked that easily if he had.

He said, 'I can satisfy anyone.'

'Did you practice?'

He nodded. 'Of course.' What a way to spend a life. Here is the kernel of Victor Graham: I can satisfy anyone. Myself, I eat potatoes. Well? He must've read something in my face because he imprisoned my fingers more severely; thank God I don't wear rings. He said, 'Do you despise me?'

'In comparison with *my* friends?' I said, and couldn't help it; I began to laugh. This pleased him.

Then I said, 'I only wish it had been more fun for you.'

'It was all right.' The cyanotic tinge was coming back but he didn't seem to feel it. 'Wasn't so easy the first few years, but when I met Val I knew I had it made. Worked like hell to get her, too.'

'You took her name?'

'No. She's old-fashioned. I used to — was able to — order her around sometimes, then . . . think we flipped a coin . . . you know, I loved her but I can't remember now.'

'And Lori?' I said.

'A beautiful child. Still a child. You'll look after her?'

'Of course.'

'This is all for her,' he said, with a stirring of the arm as if he would sweep it round him to indicate the horizon.

'She'll grow up better here,' I said.

'Sure,' he said without irony, 'and her mother'll do some work. It'll do her good. Val'll live long.' He sighed. He said, 'You should take some of this. It's religious. I feel like a Christian.'

'Instant religion? There's something like that in the trade name: Forgiveness without tears. Something. But I don't feel like forgiving anyone, you see. I'm nasty.'

What I didn't say: how dull it can become after a while, these

46

exaltations that leave nothing behind them. The headiness of anger. Perhaps I'm an addict. An anger addict. I said, 'Victor, the analgesic will last for hours, but the stimulant's wearing off. I can give you more' – holding it up – 'or you can fight it out alone, or there's this' – putting the glass ampoule by his free hand where his hand lay on the ground, that eternal mid-afternoon sun palely lighting it, the time just before the light becomes ruddy. In a few hours we would have our twilight.

'What's that?' he said. 'The ultimate analgesic?'

I think that surprised me more than his use of 'Christian.' I said, 'You clever man!'

He said, 'If you hold my hand.'

'Can't,' I said. 'It's a contact poison, works through the skin. You break the ampoule. If I held your hand I would run a considerable risk of being ultimately anesthetized myself.'

'Death's your friend,' he said.

I shook my head. 'Never!'

'Don't want it,' he said, trying to flick away the ampoule with his finger, so I rescued it – very carefully – and laid it to one side. Must remember where it is, too. Better still, pick it up and put it away in my belt. Which I did.

He said, 'I haven't been much good to Val these last months.' He was still looking straight ahead of him. He said, 'I want to see the sun,' so I turned him about with great care, Pole-wards – the sun was declining into what we had agreed to call the North, interrupted by a stumpy tree on the side of a hill. I moved him until he could see it, propping his head in my lap – he was a heavy man – I think leaving the poison with him would have been useless unless I'd put it in his hand; he was too feeble, for all his talking.

He said, 'I'm going to die.'

He was not that cyanotic. Perhaps the light concealed it, turning him rosy. This damned place has been looking stranger and stranger each morning, despite my trying not to see it that way – imagination? Like meeting a childhood friend: at first the resemblance is as clear as can be, and then after a quarter of an

47

hour, you begin to wonder. I suppose you see all the other things time has laid down on the face.

He said, 'Go away.'

I didn't move. He was breathing with difficulty. I could hear his breath stop, catch, go on, then stop again, like an electric motor with a bad connection – too apt a comparison – catch a few times, go on, stop –

I think I was hypnotized by the tree's shadow as it crawled towards us, or the shifting motes of sun in it between the leaves, the sun having sunk behind the tree and each spot of light a camera obscura of the sun: round as a coin and twinkling.

He was trying very hard to breathe. No oxygen going to that brain. Then he stopped. Easy as pie. I knew Victor was still there, shut up inside himself, but the housing was shot. No good any more. He couldn't feel anything anyone could do to it. An eerie feeling, that heavy, motionless head in my lap; you never know how mobile people are (in sleep, in hypnosis, in the deepest, drugged state) until you feel them dead. 'Dead weight' is the real thing. I know.

Two minutes.

Five . . .

Gone. The last traces died out. Only the coral shell now; the thing making it had gone somewhere else. Or anyway, wasn't here. I let his head down on to the ground – he was staring straight up – and stretched, spinning about dizzily as if for all the world I could catch him as he flew off. Catch a sight of him. There's some complicated, biochemical reason for the loss of weight at death – though it feels the opposite – but if Victor in the shape of a butterfly was zipping off to better realms, I never saw him.

The sun still hung there, behind the tree. It won't set for an hour. I've been talking into my vocoder (back in the left-hand sleeve if anyone comes) all about this. Will put it back now. Go tell everyone else, ugh.

Peaceful for the first time here. My God, how peaceful. How quiet it is. Sinful to violate that quiet.

Inconvenient to me, anyway.

Sssst! Victor!

Bon voyage.

(There's some old play where that is sung to a sinking ship, more and more merrily as the ship goes down. 'We hope you know how to swim,' they say. Perhaps we all know how to swim, by instinct, the way newborns do. They do.)

God help us, a life after *this* one?

One's enough.

They found me, they said, asleep by the (dead) body. Nathalie was very angry. They shook me awake and I stumbled and yawned back to the others; Lori was crying next to her mother while Valeria said (pushing her daughter's head into her own lap, as if blinding her), 'We want to remember him as he was.' Amazing.

The sun gone, the twilight darkened. The Smudge comes out.

As we've named it.

Day thirteen. Time to try again. Victor was put in the earth but I wasn't allowed to help – I think I've become tapu. Either that or envy. (What an extraordinary idea, planting people in the ground as if you expected them to sprout! I think they should be left about to rot, day after day, so we'd get used to it and stop being afraid of it.) When the burial party came back and the shovel was passed to Nat for digging the latrine (some more) I went and sat at her feet. I was careful about my eyes because she might throw dirt at me with the shovel – on purpose or otherwise.

I didn't say anything.

'Well?' said Nathalie, dirt-streaked, the sweat darkening in patches on her black body-suit.

'Let me dig?' I said. She leaned on the shovel, looking down at me, then turned back to her work, making the dirt fly. She was extending the pit into a shallow channel which would later be lined with something; I'm not sure what they expected to do, maybe collect fertilizer. Standing, she was above me; if she'd been down in the pit, our heads would have been on the same level.

I said, 'Just wanted to talk to you.'

Then I said, 'I envy you.'

She stopped and looked at me, nonplussed.

'I mean,' I said, 'that it must be a great simplicity. Right? A good feeling. Not being a wretched, mixed-up mess like me. I mean to face the old problems instead of the new ones, to know what the solutions are. Even though it's so hard.'

I said, 'All right, I know I'm a trial to all of you.'

Now I did not like the expression on Nathalie's face. I like to know what's coming, too. She threw down her shovel (which, hitting a projecting rock in the side of the pit, instantly unhinged itself into two separate pieces) and stood there looking at me. I wondered if Nathalie were not perhaps the Spirit of Death around here: I mean hard work, looking to the future, planning about things, that sort of stuff. She said:

'You fool.'

Then she said, *Do you think I WANT to be here!*'

'Don't – I –' I said, leaning backward. If your legs are crossed, you can't get up unless you lean forward, so I was effectively tied in a knot; if I'd got up, it would've been right into Nathalie's face.

She said, 'Oh God, you make me sick!'

I could roll sideways and get up.

'You,' she said, but her voice had changed and her eyes were no longer all pupils, so I knew she was only going to talk and I could afford to stay there, to stay helpless; she said, 'Oh, what do you know about it!'

I said, 'I'm sorry.' I looked meek. (And I was sorry, only none of them will take the cure, not one.)

She sank to her knees, but still leaning over me, which is something they teach them in government school, maybe; she said, 'Do you know where I was going before I came here?'

I shook my head.

She sat down, sort of collapsed sideways. She said, 'Well, I wasn't going to dig latrines. Or bear babies. Or plant crops.'

(There are no crops.)

'I was going,' she said, 'to school. And not to learn how to lecture on music, little woman! Something quite different.'

'Yes,' I said.

'Do you? You can't. None of you can, not even Ude; he's a paper-pusher. I wasn't; I would've learned how to kill him with my bare hands, I would have learned to make explosives – yes, even here! I would've learned how to find the right stuff and make them – and when I was finished there wasn't one of you who would have dared to come within twenty meters of me, let me tell you – and Alan would be dead.'

She pulled angrily at the grass before her, which may poison us.

'I'd love to see that other-fucker with a broken neck,' she said.

I laughed – suddenly couldn't help it. She sprang to her feet. 'Two minds with but a single thought,' I said. She sat down: very slowly, but she sat down. Loosened a little.

Nathalie smiled.

'If only we had some –' said I.

'Plaster,' she added, 'and wax, we could –'

'Make a cast –'

'Of his –'

She laughed; in fact she roared, throwing her head back. Then she said:

'And a sperm bank.' Very sober.

'There is that,' I admitted.

A short silence.

'How was Victor?' I said.

'What?' said she. 'D'you mean, was he fertile?' (They had looked at it from different viewpoints, apparently.)

She added sharply, 'How is he? He's dead!'

I stared at the ground. Earth, grass, pebbles: could've been anywhere. Nathalie got up. 'You see, one goes on,' she said. 'Unless one's afraid, like you. One learns that.'

'Afraid?' I said.

'Yes.' She strode to the pit, reached over the edge for the shovel, then straightened up and bent the thing until the handle clicked back together. With her left hand she pushed her hair behind her ears. 'You're demoralized, like all civilians,' she said. 'You miss your luxuries.'

She shoveled a spadeful of earth out on to the bank, tucked her hair behind her ears again (it always came loose and swung in her face), and leaned on the shovel: bitter, severe, very pleased with herself. She said:

'My parents were poorer than Cassie's. Did you know that? Of course not. But that's why you all need me, because I know how to fight. I didn't grow up in private, like that damn-fool little girl and I didn't grow up rich. I was in a youth group and I learned how to fight. You're bloody lucky you've got me.'

I said, 'You won a lot of scholarships, didn't you?' but she didn't like my guessing it and went back to digging, with her face set as if every bash at the dirt were at Alan-Bobby's backbone.

I said, 'Survival –' and she said, 'Survival's the name of the game. You'd better move; I'm switching to this side.' So I did.

But for what? The sound of the digging stopped; Nathalie had straightened up and was looking at me again, the death's-head.

I had spoken out loud.

I said, 'All right, all right, I didn't say it!' and scrambled to my feet. This is crazy comedy; one must, after all, do it sooner or later, and the madwoman in black is going to hit me with her shovel or fling it at my head because I want to get right in my soul before I die.

She said, 'You walking cunt, I would like to kill you, too.'

Her face is blanched to the color of paper; her eyes are black and white: all pupil. She's quite mad. If I shoot her, the others will come running. I said, 'I'll dig,' and she threw me the shovel, which did indeed almost hit me. I rapped the hinge to make sure it wouldn't fold up. Nathalie strode away over the freshly-turned dirt, head high, blazing, broadcasting hatred. 'It suits you!' she cried, meaning (I suppose) that grave-digging was my proper occupation. (It used to be taboo, like executioners.) I dug at the channel – a little sloppily, for I haven't half her purpose – and you

don't develop strength by being told off to play cards with Lori.
They had, at least, the sense to put the latrine downstream, though
the odd thing about this hole is that nobody is ever going to use it.

Did you know that hangmen were once taboo?

What do you know?

Do you know anything?

★ ★ ★

Who are you?

(I should go back and erase all that silence; the vocoder makes a
mark whenever I stop, like a punctuation mark but different; then
it begins a new line. There must be too many of them. No, hell, let
them stay. What happened later: we had our siesta; we dug some
more; Lori asked me to sing and I did, the sun hanging in the sky,
dropping no lower, remaining motionless over the same inky,
fiery, spotted bush. Silhouettes. The same long shadows from
dawn to dusk. I sang 'Chu Chu Chu'; I sang 'Love Is Splendid,
Isn't It!'; I sang 'What A Perfect Day This Has Been.' Ude had a
long conversation with Alan, who is becoming more and more
authoritative and more and more pleased with himself. They
spoke in low voices; I couldn't hear what they said. Making plans?

(We lay down to sleep.)

By writ and tort, by hullaballoo and brouhaha, I declare this
tape-deck locked to all voice-prints but mine, locked *re* playback,
locked *re* print-out, and may God have mercy on your soul.

So be it.

Day twenty. Eighteen. Nineteen? I can't remember. Too much
going on. Managing people is a melancholy skill; it depends
mostly on keeping your mouth shut.

The night after we'd buried Victor Graham I took off with the
broom and the face-mask, making up a package of food, soap, a
mattress, bits of plastic towelling, spare underwear, things like

53

that, all tied up in a sheet with one set of corners tied above the other. I went upstream. I got up in the middle of the night and used up the last of my sleepydust, spraying them as if I'd been putting *Grow* on plants, tomato beds perhaps, stepping carefully between them as you would between your eggplants or your cantaloupe vines, then taking the broomstick low above the water, for the ground-effect leaves a trail: some crushed things don't rise and over bare earth there's a characteristic sort of smudge: loose stuff blown to both sides like a giant broom. So they might find me.

I went up two hundred and forty kilometers, until I hurt all over, until the river cut between sharper and sharper hills like glacial debris and glacial scaur: an old garbage-heap that glaciers push in front of them and leave behind when they retreat. Until the river went down between two hills and vanished, down into the ground.

I found a cave. The drop to the water: twenty meters, the other bank almost flat. A streamlet three fingers across rising in the loose rock-rubble in the back and making straight for the edge, with the necessary number of curlicues to avoid stones and hillocks. Beyond, a steep hill covered with thorny tangle, something new, like blackberry vines, and the cave not really a cave but an accidental hole-in-a-heap with boulders wedged together and stuff grown over the top. But very big, very solid boulders. The streamlet-bottom is pebbles, fine gravel. I put everything down and poked assiduously in the rubbish in back with the broomstick handle and even lit a fire with some of the litter found outside, thrusting burning stuff into the back of the cave in several places.

Nothing. No alarums and excursions, no nasty little dwellers with pincers, no alarmed rustlings, no sound, no motion.

So there's only people.

I'm about one-point-fifty meters tall; the cave is about one-point-sixty-five and I like that. Tall people can't stand upright here. I propped the broomstick against the drift of friable rock and harder pebbles at the back, put down my hobo's bundle, unrolled the mattress, and laid my things out. The extra underwear I'd put in the metal box I once used to store my music tapes; this is where the vocoder print-out will go (when I make a print-out). I guess we will bury it. There was room for my mattress at the edge, to one side of the little, bisecting stream: bed, running water, and I can hear in the directions I can't see. The streamlet makes almost no noise: too tiny. Wonderful for sanitation. And it didn't kill me. I had gone two hundred and forty kilometers, perhaps a hundred sixty as the crow flies (none here), and that's six or seven days' walking for exceedingly determined people.

And that is why I carried nine days' food.

But I lost track. I thought they'd gone away. I went out scouting with the broomstick and saw no one, not from the tops of the highest hills. I couldn't go too far or I'd lose my way back – until I thought of spreading some underwear under two rocks; you can see the white very far.

There was nobody coming, no black specks, no swaying in the bushes, not even three-quarters of the way down the river. It was altogether beautiful. But I couldn't go any closer. Wouldn't. Didn't want to. Didn't dare.

So I lost track.

They came in the afternoon. Putting one's head down close to the stream, you can just barely hear it talking, but I think I screened out everything else with the river because I never heard them. I woke from a dream of talking very rationally to Cassie somewhere utterly indistinct and uncharacterized (so that it might have been equally easily back on the ship or in the middle of the Grand Canyon) and there she was, standing in silhouette in the door of the cave; I was mucking about in the floating layers between light sleep and lighter sleep when you become aware of your body and don't want to, like anesthetic: places in the mattress that weren't as thick as they should be. Stretching. Stiff back.

I said, 'Why have you come for the water thingie? I left it.'

I woke up.

Why didn't they come in? Because they couldn't see in, probably. I had thought Cassie was already inside, but as my vision came back I realized I'd only been asleep; everything's flat for a moment after you wake up.

I said, 'How'd you find me?'

She said, 'I want to talk to you. Can I come in?' Brave Cassandra! — whose shaky voice indicated something else was going on. Probably Alan-Bobby exploring the hillside. There are heavy scramblings overhead, something rather large and stupid moving about on the cave roof. Either he's proving himself for Lori or (more likely) they decided he was It. I propped the mattress (which is very thin and light) against the rock-rubble at the back of the cave; don't want to trip on it.

I said, 'Good Lord, you didn't bring Lori, did you?'

'No, she's with Val.' So it's Val now. I said, 'I don't know what you're doing here and I don't know what you want of me. Go away.'

She said, 'Can't you come out for a minute?'

I let a moment go by. 'All right,' I said. I suppose one of us has to act in good faith that the other is in good faith, slender as such a chance may be. Let's test it. I put on my jacket, picked up a couple of rocks about the size of my hand. Circled close to the cave wall, on the side Cass was on so she couldn't see me, watching my feet carefully, and made it almost to the entrance without making too much noise. Which I hoped sounded like echoes, anyhow. Still in shadow. I threw one of the rocks across the cave and it made a very satisfactory, verisimilar sort of sound, falling in the loose shale over there, and there was a truly tremendous scramble from above, as Alan-Bobby the Megatherium dropped from the cave roof and rushed inside.

And bashed his head against the ceiling. He does not realize, I think, just how expendable the others consider him to be. On his hands and knees, shaking his head from side to side. Then he fell into the streamlet. He couldn't see very well, of course. And the others might not have told him to do this; he might be acting on his own. It's possible. I threw the other rock at the back of the cave and when he turned to follow the sound of where it landed – I think he was still dizzy – I had meant to give him a shot of something. I did. I really did. But there was no time. And I knew I must not let him touch me; then he'd know where I was. So I picked up another rock, picking up something in my head that wasn't mine, too, that I still don't know, and before he could get up, I hit him down and down again, just above the ear.

Concussion, at best.

So there's no going back.

'Alan?' said Cassie.

Nathalie, John, Cassie. If no Val. I kept quiet. Cassie stepped out of my view and there was some sort of parley out there, little whisperings and scufflings about.

'Hello in there!' said John Ude.

I said nothing, 'What do you want?' being a question that in this case seemed rather obvious.

'Hello?' he said.

I cried, 'You've got the water-cycler, for God's sake, you've got it!'

He said, 'But we want you back. We like your singing.'

I said, 'John, I only want to be by myself. I'll give you the broomstick; I can push it out.'

'Alan?' said someone, a woman's voice.

'Hibernating,' I said. 'Out like a light. Your Hero bashed his head against the ceiling, which is very low. Showing his usual intelligence, which is likewise. If you'll stand away from the entrance, I'll push out the broomstick. No, I'll break it, that's better. Ruin it. Push out the pieces. That way nobody has it, you see?' There's probably someone else on the roof, but I can't see the shadow. If I were there myself, I'd wait until I saw somebody come out, then jump them, maybe push them off the edge. There's an old trick with a hat, but I haven't got a hat. My ears all on edge waiting to hear Alan-Bobby stir, wishing he would, wishing he wouldn't. I said, 'Stand where I can see you.'

Cassie moved into view in the cave opening on one side, Ude on the other.

'And . . . ?' (said I).

'Nath is ill,' he said. 'We left her back home.' Back *home*! And Val and Nath and Cass – what a lot of intimacy has been developing in the last few days! I decided to believe him, or pretend that I believed him, or act as if I were pretending that I did believe him. If there's a fight, I might get broken. So I stepped into the sunlight at the mouth of the cave – but not quite out – until my eyes got accustomed to the light; it was a shock to see them looking so grubby, so angry. They must've been drinking river water on the long march up.

I said foolishly, 'What've you been drinking?'

'The same as you,' said John Ude, 'see?' and he held up something that caught the sun and sparkled wonderfully. 'Compass,' he said. 'Bet you didn't know. There's a magnetic field, all right. And you forgot that Nath was up this way before. We came overland.' Then he yelled 'Now!' and somebody dropped on me from above as he grabbed me, both together, Nathalie undoubtedly because it smelled like her, not that I'd ever noticed before. Fallen on sloppily, *thud!* with my face in the dust because I hadn't had the sense to duck, and thinking only it was so odd that I did know what Nathalie smelled like.

'Let her up,' said Ude. Big man. 'Cass, go get Alan.' So I suppose Cassie went inside. I was not going to turn around to see; don't want to get my back to the edge. I heard her moving around tentatively in there. Looked up so very carefully, hugging the ground: the woman to one side, the man to the other. Two bureaucrats. Looking up makes me dizzy.

I started to cry. Because we never could be friends, I suppose. Cassie would be blinded by the dark, but not for long. There wasn't much time. He leaned over me, the silly way you do when you think you've got somebody down; he put his hands on his hips and with as much angry relish as if he'd been talking to the whole damned planet itself, he said, 'You're mad. Did you know that? We're going to tie you to a tree with your hands behind so you can't get loose. We can never trust you again.'

I pulled his feet out from under him. He sat, or went down backwards along the ledge (I don't know which) and I turned and shot in Nathalie's direction, not even seeing her, not knowing if it would miss her or not.

But she was awfully close.

Gas-guns don't make noise.

I shot at him without seeing him. Following my motion with my eyes a moment later to see him – I think he was hit in the knee or something – clutching one thigh and standing on the other foot. There was a great roar behind me, pebbles and boulders going over the edge down the bank. I shot him again, aiming this time, and – once he fell – kicked him down the slope. Another landslide.

There was no one on top of the cave, no one on the hill. I suppose Val really hadn't come. I felt even dizzier and waited on the empty ledge without standing up for Cass to come out with the broom-stick, or discover Alan with his head beaten in and scream – and was he alive? And what would she do? And what would I do then?

She came out empty-handed. No, with a rock in one hand. Blood on it. She dropped it to the ground with exaggerated calm, wiped her hands on her sheet-made-into-a-dress, and sat down cross-legged on the bare earth, which she did with astonishing gracefulness. Something to do with having been a dancer once, I suppose. Anyway, Cassie hadn't wasted love on any of them.

'Well!' she said, peering over the edge, 'you have been going it, haven't you? Someone ought to give you a medal.' She licked her index finger, then tapped her own shoulder with her third finger. 'Run home before it dries.'

I said nothing.

She remarked conversationally, 'The prof person said you'd be up here. You know, along the water somewhere. Frankly, you should have gone a lot farther away. A hell of a lot farther. That's what I would have done. I told them to let you alone.'

I said, 'Cassandra —'

She said, 'I know, I know. If I had a baby, it would die. And if it didn't, I would die. Anyway, my Ma had me by Caesarean.'

She said, 'I could tell you all about it, the kind of anesthetic, the scars, the stitches. God knows I heard about it enough.' She laughed. Swaggering Cassandra, the beautiful waitress, born to be a star, born to be a loser, doesn't know that hard births don't run in families. Not as simply as that.

'Oh damn them!' she said. 'Damn them, don't they ever even come back to *look*?'

I shook my head.

She said, 'What do we do now? Fight to the death? Like stupid Nathalie, who thought she was a man?' A social solecism Valeria Victrix would never have perpetrated, despite her being a Mrs. But in Cassie's terms Cassie is right, I suppose.

'Here,' she said harshly, making me jump, 'give me that,' and reaching out in an absurdly unbalanced position, she had the gas-gun in her hand and was trying to get her fingers round it. It's a flat, half-shapeless piece, because it's designed to be hidden, and you have to know how to use it. I shut my eyes. 'Careful!' Not like this.

'Give me that stuff,' said Cassandra the brava. 'Right now.'

'What?' I said, opening my eyes.

'That stuff you're always carrying,' she said sharply. 'You've got it about you somewhere. You're too much of a coward to be without it.' She turned red. 'Trust you not to go around without carrying every kind of poison there is, you viper! Always wants a way out, doesn't she? Give it!'

So I did. I popped from my belt two pellets, which I put on the ground between us under those angry, angry eyes, two greenish-grey, extra-special, euphoric exits that looked just like Cassie's eyes. They fetched a great deal in the market once. And are fetching a great deal right now.

I said, 'Please don't throw that down.' I meant the gun. She put it more carefully down in the dust between us. I watched her pick up the pills. I think I was shaking. Something – not me – said, 'Cassandra, I would be very pleased to share your company. Very grateful.'

'I ought to poison your water,' she said, 'but I won't. I'll go do it somewhere else. What do you do? Swallow them?'

I nodded. She was showing off again, Cassie the 3-D Cat, Cassie the actress.

'Now you can go kill Lori,' she said. She started to pick her way sideways over the hill, a little ageing in her imitation peplum or whatever it was. Then she stopped, and turned back, and smiled.

'Honored to share my company, huh?' she said. She added:

'For how many years?'

Then she went away.

Alan-Bobby was dead. No pulse in his groin, no chest movement. I used the broomstick to haul Nathalie's and John Ude's bodies from the stream-bed, one at a time, and take them a good km or so downstream; they could rot there. Dead people are like sandbags but in odd shapes because they keep folding up, and because they were still warm; I kept getting irritated at them for flinging their arms and legs out like that and not helping me. I think that's characteristic. I left Alan alone, because I was tired, and decided to go downstream. From high enough (I was not stuck with the water now) you can see the river winding like a silver snake in the distance and the grey-green brush folded over on itself in hill after hill, each darker and stranger than the last; plum-colored at the horizon. League upon league. A rumpled, painted tablecloth where the glaciers had come down. I went down by the side of the stream this time and much straighter, leaving a snake of flattened vegetation over the hills. Watch it after you pass and you can see it slowly straighten up.

I had to go down.

Otherwise they might have to decide to come up to me.

No stops this time.

*

I left the broom by the stream and far enough away; nobody's going to steal it or break it or hit me over the head with it. I slept for a while; it was going to start greying-out soon. I ate the stuff I'd brought with me, a kind of candy bar and then something salty you mix with water and which I'd mixed and carried in the plastic wrapping, but that had got all over itself and on to my jacket pocket. Supposed to be soup, anyway, not paste. I tried to wipe it off with the plastic but it was very uncomfortable: beginning to go stiff. When it dries, it'll fall off. (Most of it.)

Then we sit.

Where is Val?

There are bushes, trees, the marks of feet. I can't smell the latrine. There are long, flattened smudges on the ground where things have been dragged. Do I remember how to get to the new camp?

Where's Cassie?

It all looks familiar, but then everything here looks familiar. Follow the water (again). I kept it in sight, trying to hide behind bushes. There were more footprints, a kind of confused scramble and crossing of marks, a place very much walked on.

I saw something white between the trees. That's not a natural color. A little closer: someone had tied a sheet to the edge of the old bungalow, for a lean-to. Very sensible. But there's nobody there. Doesn't seem to be anyone about.

Valeria came out of the bungalow, flapping a towel in her hands as if to dry it or shake crumbs off it. Then she hung it on one of the sticks that made up the lean-to. She stared into the distance, almost as if she'd seen me, then turned and went slowly back into the bungalow, only to come out again a moment later with another towel draped over her arm. Oddly: it covered her hand. She walked idly forward, looking at nothing, short Val, old Val, her hair grey at the roots, not in her royal-blue sari and her earrings now but in somebody's cast-off khaki trousers and a white shirt. The curve of her back near the neck is very much exaggerated by age; that's called 'dowager's hump.' Nothing balances on the spine quite as it used to twenty years before. The opposite posture from what soldiers used to do or at least were supposed to do.

She was perhaps nine meters from me, still without purpose, still peering about, when I realized she had seen me from the first. Must've. She was faking. The towel dropped and Val Victrix was holding a gun. Revolver, I think. She walked closer and stopped at twice conversational distance. She looked as if she had just noticed me. Then she said:

'You're not coming near my child!'

I said, 'It's all right, Val. The others are coming. They're not using the broom because Nat's got a broken ankle.'

'Oh, did you give it to her?' she said, enjoying herself. 'And tell me why Nath would walk with a broken ankle?'

'And why they'd trust you alone?' she added. It was a revolver, no question. I said quickly:

'How is Lori? You know how much I care about Lori.'

'I won't let you near her!'

'All right,' I said. 'My goodness.'

Silence. Mrs Graham is running out of melodramatic things to say. After a moment she remarked, 'This has still got all its bullets, you know, sixteen of them,' so if she were lying I might get her to use up the ammunition, but then again she might use it up in me.

She said, 'When we took Lori from the crèche, she was such a little thing. And so beautiful, so tiny, but you wouldn't know that. You wouldn't know anything. No one does, not even my husband. That's right, even Victor. And you don't know how to live, my girl, you really don't. Take it from one who does.'

Who hid that gun? Whose gun is it?

'It's tragic to think,' said Mrs Gee cheerfully, and by this I deduced that power was making her talky, 'that when we die here, you'll never have lived but I will. Think of that.'

I thought about it, conscientiously. No one has listened to this woman for weeks so that thing in her hand is a compulsory Ear; it means I must listen and she likes that. She went on:

'How much money do I have?'

None now, of course.

'You don't even know,' (she said amused). 'Well, I'll tell you. Six mill a month. Eurodollar. That puts me in the top one-tenth of the top one percentile, I believe. And I'm in the credit economy, too – I'm not a civilian, you know, not legally – and with a credit-level-one you can have anything you want in this world, anything at all.'

This world? Goodness!

'Clothes? No!' (she went on) 'Food? Service? No! That's just ordinary life. You grubby little people think "Mrs Graham" is foolish, don't you? And maybe you think it's foolish and strange and rich to buy a man and strange and foolish and rich to buy a child, but one gets sick of renting people and even sicker of renting pets – it's dull – and I don't enjoy politics and there's one thing about bought people if you're wise: they stay bought. You can't have it both ways but I can: the old *and* the new.'

It must be new money. The politesse isn't there. The taking for granted. Or has she just gone a little batty these last few weeks? She smiled. She said, 'My friends think I'm quite eccentric, did you know that?'

Then she said, in an altered tone of voice, 'I didn't buy Lori for myself, you know. I thought I would but it didn't work out like that. She was an awfully sick little thing; she needed money like mine. That's why I chose her. Well, one reason. Do you know how many operations that child's had? She was hooked to a kidney machine when I first saw her and she needed a heart implant. And dozens of things. They said the only things that really worked were her central nervous system and her skeletal muscles. The surgeon said she had actually become immunized against herself in several ways; we almost didn't lick that one. And I did it, I did all of it, I paid for it myself and every bit of it on P.D. too so she wouldn't have to be there while they were doing it to her! Otherwise it would have killed her. Even so I think it might have had some bad effects; psychic displacement can play hell with the mind if you're not careful. A sort of backlash, they say. But we had the best, the very best.' She laughed. 'That child cost as much money as a small New England state. Believe it. I don't quarrel with Cass, but to have a baby and call yourself a mother – ! One doesn't say such things, of course. One doesn't quarrel. Not here. But having children . . . '

She looked at me, quite scornful and very happy, still holding the gun. She said:

'Victor fell in love with her. That was a good thing, of course. A sick child – well, it does something to you. To have her around. After a while. I love her too. It gets to you, you know.'

'Of course,' I said.

She said, 'I did it. I am the real mother here.' Then she said, 'That's all I'm going to tell you about myself. I don't think you'd understand the rest. It's very odd for me to be here with all of you, but of course one tries to make do. To be polite. And of course you'll tell no one what I've told you.'

'Of course not,' I said, immensely relieved.

'Because I shall kill you right now,' said Valeria Graham.

As if on cue, from back in the bungalow, came a faint 'Motherrrrr!' – but this ghastly screech, which we should not have been able to hear at all, is merely Lori's I-mean-business voice, the voice of a handsome tarsier or a pretty macaque monkey possessed by demons. Such an expensive life. Smiling tenderly (and just a little self-consciously dramatically) Valeria Graham motioned me away from the bungalow and farther into the trees. She put the forefinger of her free hand to her lips: Lori must not hear it. Lori must not find the body. We all know that child's preternatural hearing. Val is too close to me. I fell to the ground, roaring 'Lori! Help! Lori! Help!' and trying to roll towards the mother. There's a shot *blam!* in here somewhere, and I can't hear a thing, deafened, grabbing her ankles, only I haven't got proper leverage and she won't fall all the way down. She gets on her knees, steadying herself with one hand, and points the gun a hand's-width from my face, happily ready to shoot me.

I grabbed the barrel and snapped it around so the gun was

pointing at Mrs Graham's white shirt – she didn't seem to understand that you must hold a gun rigidly, like an extension of your arm – and either the motion pulled the trigger or she pulled the trigger or something pulled the trigger or at any rate the little machine went off again.

She collapsed slowly sideways with only a very little blood in the front. A big slug like that makes one jump, first. Odd thing to see. They must've left the gun with her, for protection.

She never fired a gun before in her life.

Dead. Or near it. The revolver fallen on the ground. I picked it up and ran towards the bungalow. Lori is going from screeching to downright squealing; this is her you-must-attend-to-me-right-away-or-else voice. I sprinted the last few meters and fetched up breathless against the bungalow doorway. Couldn't see a thing at first and then even when I could there was no Lori, only an odd, dark shape showing on one of the bunks.

It was her back.

She was sitting up in the bunk, wrapped in one of her Mommy's royal-blue-and-gold saris, with Mommy's card deck made-from-sheets more or less on her knees and (I think) on the bed around her. Her legs were crossed. She leaned forward, putting one card on top of another somewhere in her lap. She said:

'I'm not coming outside; I don't care if it is healthy.'

You must not shoot a Lori with a large-caliber revolver. It's not right. I shifted Mrs Gee's gun to my left hand but quietly, quietly. You must not shoot an ebony-haired Lori.

'Hello,' I said.

That impossible child did not even turn round. She only said:

'What an awful noise! What were you doing?'

'Target practice,' I said.

'I wish you'd shoot Mother,' said the Lori absently. There was a moment's silence. Then she added, 'Mother keeps telling me I must be careful. Careful, careful. I'm tired of being careful. I think Mother is over-protective. Don't you agree?'

'No,' I said.

66

'Oh, go away,' said the Lori, 'you're revolting' and she put a card on another card. I shot her in the back of the head. Did it with the gas-gun, shrugging it from my sleeve, practically touching her hair. There is a kind of swooshing sound as the bullet explodes within. She slumped forward to one side, against the wall, her crossed legs keeping her half-upright. I thought I might gather up the cards and take them with me, but I didn't. No reason to, after all.

Felt nothing.

Odd, to feel nothing.

She might want the cards back. She might come for them.

I went outside and sat, thinking. Woke near dawn. It was like the first time I'd fled – only then they were all alive – and the problem was, what about the water-cycler? I mean this is what I had thought, under that awful heaven, more than a little dazed, trying to move about in the near-dark and not step on anyone – I mean didn't I have a moral right to take the water-recycler because they were trying to colonize, which would require them to drink the water raw, and here all I wanted was to starve comfortably to death? But they would be awfully mad if I took it, which might send them after me, though they might come after me anyway, and I could leave a note on playing cards: *Will send broomstick back walking speed* – but that'll give them my direction if this place has a magnetic field to make the compass gyro work and if not it'll get joggled and move off somewhere else. Or I could leave a sketch of a still: *Ord. wood fire deform plastic tumblers, water in here* (arrow). It wouldn't be poisonous. We'd been using boiling water in the tumblers over and over again.

I had thought a great deal about these things that night, on my knees, staring straight ahead, probably having breathed in some of the sleepygas I had puffed at the others. Very vague in the head. It occurred to me (then) that I could hold the water-cycler in my lap, but I would first have to unscrew the coupling to the storage tank; so I did and sat with the cycler in my lap on the broomstick, and fastened my belt around the cycler. Just fitted. (Now.)

That was the first trip. What you might call a rehearsal for the second. Much like the second.

Find the broom, stumbling in the dark, water-cycler cradled in one arm, harder this time because it's upstream, put on the dust-mask, flip *Go* and *Rise*, make the little toggles all *Manual*, and point Polewards. Silly to say North. Swing round, sending dust over everything (is it dryer than it was before?) and make a broad loop towards the Equator; you want to find bare rock because the mask is getting clogged and this time no forced-draught mist from the river, either. Over the hills and through the woods, dead dark blots against the ordinary darkness: these must be trees. (The first time I went carefully Equator-wards over the hill Victor had died on.) An old, old tune through my head, pre-Modern music:

> We're off!
> We're off!
> We're off in a motor car!
> There's fifty coppers
> After us
> And we don't know where we are!

How extraordinarily silly. Yet the first time there'd been joy in it. I went slowly at first, on account of the dark, and the cycler pushing its angles into me in the very worst places. The broom was going perhaps twenty-three kph. Nothing about the country-side changed and I was afraid I'd get lost because I wasn't riding right over the water (like the first time) so I turned left, refastening my belt around the cycler (this time).

Then I waited. (Both times. The first time I made a great loop Equator-wards, to find bare rock, not to leave a trail.)

One does see, really, in the dark. If you wait long enough. Not real dark, underground dark. But even in a bare night you can see if you wait long enough. Just don't look directly at things. You can even tell water from non-water.

So I knew it must be dawn. And speeded up a little — which lifted me a little, though it never goes far, not much above knee-high – and knew I was going towards the Pole, which is the opposite way from The Smudge this time of night. And when I realized it was indeed that greyish, crepuscular, eye-swarming, can't-see time, I checked the switches on the broom to make sure I had done it properly by feel the first time (both times).

The first time I had had the brilliant idea of riding over the water itself, following the stream up to wherever it began, for I would have to have water, and though the ground-effect makes a sort of immense trough in the water (a mist-shower which wets you all over and you have to take off your shoes and roll up your clothes to your knees; still it's like riding in air-and-water mixed) the second time I followed by the side of the stream and evened out a lot of the windings by staying on the rising bank because it didn't matter. I dragged my legs in the brush. And so on. And on. Endless twilight. Things swimming about greyly, like riding through an aquarium. Water to the eye. It got chillier and chillier. I've kept my watch; it can't tell time in the usual sense because one really doesn't give a damn about the standard day, but there are other uses: timing one's pulse, the length of the day, even the turning of the stars.

Aren't any. (Only planets.)

Ah, yes, there's one. I saw it prepare endlessly to rise; everything grew more distinct (but was all the same countryside: little hills, brushy scrub, low trees) and after many hours, which I did not bother to time, and after I dozed, for I don't remember when the color came back to things, I saw our single star – I mean our sun – rise slowly but very visibly because at these latitudes its track around the sky is so low that it rises perceptibly sideways.

It got warmer.

The first time I'd pushed myself; second time no reason. I stopped whenever I began to nod. I stopped to relieve myself. I just stopped. Wading in the stream, sun dries your feet afterwards. Just sitting. Even without that preposterous object in my lap with its cubical-but-too-many-corners balancing act, one's bottom hurts, eventually, and one's back; it took hours and hours. All times the light was the same, the sun at the same height in the sky always; there were no bird sounds, no insect sounds, no animal sounds; it's all the same always, only around the rim of this enormous stage-set there is a spotlight that swings slowly around to my back.

The stream got deeper. The countryside got a little dryer and rockier.

And how I liked it! I haven't moved this fast in a long time. It unwinds like a highway, faster than funicular, faster than a bicycle, almost as fast as an electric car, it's like walking effortlessly, gliding on someone else's feet, like museum exhibits in which you sit in an armchair and are carried effortlessly past miniatures of subterranean cities, underwater farms, the interiors of fusion plants, the lunar mountains, observatories and colonies on Mars, on the solar planets, among the asteroids, even alien landscapes, imaginary landscapes.

Even

Well, it was pretty. It was pretty enough. It got rockier and more hilly. The ground sprouted patches of something new that eventually joined into a complete ground-cover: tangles and barbs like blackberry brambles (which meant I had to wear my shoes) and the right-hand bank of the stream got higher and higher. The stream grew narrower and deeper. As I said, it was like going from the hills of an ancient flood-plain (roundish and low, not the sharp crumple of a rock layer pushed up from below) into glacial debris and glacial scaur; what this is, really, is an old garbage-heap which the glaciers pushed in front of them like a land-scow and then left behind.

I say it resembles this.

But pretty. Very pretty. Water started to come down from here and there on the high bank, streamlets big as a finger, mere drip-drops, mistfalls that evaporated halfway to the surface of the river — these can't be rain-fed, not here — and the first and second time I was making silly pictures in my mind of jungled and trellised interior pipes, real ones of metal or baked porcelain (with

70

flanges) which had been broken up by the glaciers, and that was why the water began indignantly seeping to the surface or springing up here and there. The air was very dry, though, all the same. There ought to be monkeys, orchids, brilliant birds, canoes full of native heroes. Both times I turned aside at a fairly big waterfall-let, maybe three fingers across, and steered with difficulty up the steep bank (the stick turns over if you try to send it up a too-steep grade).

This is my cave. Nice things: mattress, little bisecting stream, metal box, extra underwear, some food, the vocoder. And so on. Very nice.

Well, I told you all about that.

Inside is something very unpleasant, unless he's got up and walked away.

Oh, he hasn't.

I really didn't want to go in. I don't mean anything rational; it just kept turning me away.

I said, 'Look here, it's *my* cave. You get out.'

He was so dead. Like a statue: cold as marble but made of rubber and everything stiff and at strange angles, with this Godawful picture of death imprinted on it. I can't say I cared to look at him. And had to clean the cave floor, too.

The broom will never hold us both; he's too heavy. He's taking up a lot of room in my home, besides, and that's irritating. So finally I strapped him on the broom with my belt and tied him on, too, with strips of sheeting, and pointed the whole mess over the edge of the bank. The broomstick rolled end over end down the bank – I was afraid it would catch in a sidewise position and just lie there, pushing – but it wobbled upright like a live thing when it reached flatter ground (I thought I might have to go fix it) and began to ascend the other bank, a little drunkenly. His legs were catching in underbrush and making the thing jerk. But it smoothed out when it hit flat ground and up the hill and over the top, smoothly and efficiently, the way it's supposed to, and unless Alan-Bobby falls off (can't hold on; he's dead) it's off for a jaunt around the world, in the opposite direction to the sun.

So if Alan-Bobby is going West, then the sun is rising in the West and setting in the East or we are really near the South Pole and not the North Pole, and he's going East and the sun's going East-to-West.

Only names, only names.

On the way up I saw, lying among the bushes, Cassie's white peplum. I think Cassie was inside it.

Oh, yes, I forgot to tell you . . .

I know she was; I saw her. Wanted to circle around her and didn't. She was lying on her back, limbs a little sprawled, staring at the sun, and something uncharacteristic in the air (for there are few breezes here) was moving some strands of her hair up and forward over her face, up and forward, over and over again. I've seen people who died using that stuff; they usually lie down and are happy long before the end. I wondered what would've happened to her if.

Please, I'd like to take another flight; this one doesn't fit my tour. Can't I have another flight? I want to get my hair done at the hotel.

Alan-Bobby has gone to see the world. Lori is playing cards in Heaven. I'm not alone yet, but when the broom wears out and crashes (where?), when he falls off, when the bodies rot with their own internal bacteria, when they're all gone, when Lori is dust and Valeria earth, when Alan-Bobby moulders and sinks into some other continent, when Nathalie and John are bones in water and then air and then nothing, then I'll be alone. When Cassie is only a white flag, a shred of artificial silk, bits of sheeting abraded to powder and sunk into the ground, a few fibers slowly settling into the ground around the roots of plants.

Then I'll be alone.

I'm alone.

Now I'll tell you about the first time. My four or five good days. When I woke up my watch had stopped; I must have slept long. It's the old-fashioned kind that winds itself up by the movements of your arm, which means that once a month you shake your arm vigorously, but I think the water had got to it. Ah, why didn't you buy one with a sealed power-source, as everyone told you to? (Because they're expensive.) Not that it mattered. I made a sun-dial from a thing like a twig, just stuck it in a patch of bare ground out in front of the cave. I'd fallen asleep before I'd marked where the sun went down (and comes up); so I had no landmark for it . . . thing *like* a twig.

They're succulents. This was a shock. I went out very carefully from the cave because I didn't want to fall and break some part of me as I'm very likely to do because my footing is never very good. I scrambled up the slope outside, trying not to touch anything in the rubbish. They looked like the downstream trees: low, silvery, a sort of grey-green. The 'silvery' was probably hairs, like a cactus. I don't think any of us ever noticed. Succulents are water-conservers; they're relatives of cacti, and that should mean there's going to be a very hot summer. Or a very long summer. Or a dry summer. Or no winter.

What do these trees do in winter?

Answer: they walk to the Equator. Well, maybe they do. This is not in the least like New Jersey. I used to have a potted plant called Hen-and-Chickens, a little pot of it, and they felt just like this: tough, elastic pillows. But these are much flatter. There's no join between stem and branch, as if they didn't ever fall off the way deciduous leaves do, though from a short distance away they look wonderfully alike. I thought to myself that I should not touch anything – allergic poisons? Just plain poisons? No way to tell.

The light may be turning them grey, except at sunrise or sunset. It's a pale, whitish, Northern sunlight, the way I remember Canada. Oddly wintry for such an outwardly amiable place; during the day the light is winter and the plants are tropical but it's dry, very dry; this does in a mild, subtle, discordant way what the night sky – which I am going to be careful never to see again – does so horribly, so insistently.

I don't want to look at The Smudge ever again.

From inside the cave one can see the ledge stretching about a meter to the edge of the cliff and then the lower bank, some twenty meters away, and more low, irregular hills beyond, close enough to enact a very satisfactory imitation of mountains. Deal with things a little at a time. It's a pretty landscape. An imitation or remembrance of mountains.

One thing at a time.

I went out and sat on the edge of the cliff, my feet dangling, chunking stones into the river. If I were a geologist (I mean a planetologist) I might've known what kind they were. There are no traces on either bank of the river's ever having been higher than it is now, so either it was at its height now and would go down later or it would never go down. Which is odd, when you think of the succulents. (Which grow right down to the bank and did downstream, too, as far as I remembered.) Which should be storing water but they're flat. Therefore they aren't storing water, at least not yet. So the river will rise or it'll rain or something before they stoke up for the drought. But the river's never been higher. So it won't ever rise. So the succulents don't know what they're doing.

I went back inside and arranged my calendar: a cleared place with one pebble *squat!* on the earth. Day One. Simple. I set up the water-cycler in the back of the cave, where the stream comes out of the rocks and I had a jolly time getting the tripod level. Then took the clothes out of the metal box and put my extra clothes on top, and the soap, and the food. Just a pair of shorts and a shirt, really, and an all-over undie. Had a fit of the giggles (Elaine On Desert Island – of which there are none on Earth that do not contain resort hotels – her 3-D viewer, her burning-glass, her resourcefulness, ages eight to twelve). I had to stay up until sunset so I could mark where sunset was – and wouldn't you know the blasted astronomical event happened right in back of the cave? So I had to climb the hill to get a decent look at it; it was either that or back right off the ledge. Then I ducked inside and went to sleep really quick. I didn't start a fire with my lighter, no need, though Elaine had a pocket lighter. (Would've probably burned myself up.) It was my little apartment. My little hotel. I had a dream full of echoes; I was standing alone on an empty stage, under one spotlight, singing with immense power and élan:

When I'm calling yoo-hoo-hoo-hoo-hoo-hoo-hoo

There was Pebble Two after Pebble One. When the sun was over a particular fold in the hills, marked also by a tree on the opposite bank, I put a pebble down. It's midday. In this thirty-hour (?) day I sleep twice, once through the dusk, the night, the dawn, once in the middle of the afternoon. It suits. I like watching my little amphitheatre change, the shadows wheel obediently around the trees, the sundial reach 270 degrees (or thereabouts), everything begin to turn orange. I slept a lot and sang a lot, the first time. I knew I wouldn't sleep more than ten hours a night, more than two or three hours in the day. I never used to have sleep enough, always had to get up for something-or-other, I could never sleep long enough. Dreadful mornings shivering and cold, hours and hours to real waking time. Evenings when I lay in bed wakeful and desperate. I always wanted to sleep 'til noon, sleep 'til one, then get up and find it morning. Now I do. No standard time here. The sun was no lower, the place it rose and the place it set no farther apart. Pebble Three. Pebble Four.

Maybe it takes years for the summer solstice here.

Which was when I lost track.

Second time, I had to clean up, gather dried blood clinging to dirt in my extra shirt and throw it over the ledge. Put the mattress back where it'd been, put the water-recycler back up. The first time I came here I said out loud, 'I'm alone!' but the second time makes this a very crowded little cave. Nothing to do about it, only wait; they'll fade; they'll go away. I felt like an interior decorator the first time, such glee.

(Why didn't I go back and circle around Cassie? Didn't, though. Now I want to go back.)

One thing at a time.

I re-set my calendar. Filled the water-cycler again from the little stream in the cave; then put my shorts, my shirt, my all-over undie in a corner, folded up. Very neat. Pulled the mattress about and took some pebbles out from under it. I'll leave the other rocks and pebbles – I'll have to do something with them later. Boring otherwise.

And I talked all this out into the vocoder, ate, defecated into the stream (which takes an hour or so, busily running, to deal with it), woke, dozed, slept a lot. Fell asleep in the afternoon and had a long, inconclusive dream about Alan-Bobby in which he came back (in the dream) and we had a fight or anyway something was very boring and very wrong. Woke up stiff. The mattress feels harder this time.

I shall be bored to death long before I starve. The sun is up longer, if possible, or at least no less, and rising and setting no farther apart, so maybe it will be hotter. The daylight longer. Maybe there will be no night at all. I got very hungry (food all gone) and I think my stomach was preparing to eat itself, but if you've dieted, you know this quiets down after the first few days. I drank a lot of water (which I knew I would) and it didn't help (as I knew it wouldn't). On a diet you do everything you can to keep your spirits up. The neo-Christians had a way of coping with boredom by meditation but if you do that you're apt to get hallucinations instead. How interesting.

Just realized: I am fasting like a Desert Father, so in a few days I'll have hallucinations anyway. It is a driving, driving: to get food.

My cross is gone, you know? my cross is gone, my cross is gone, I can't wear it, O dammit, dammit, why didn't I keep it?

Well, let's get on with it.

It's boring. So boring. Pebble Three. I'll tell you about the neo-Christians; they're nobody. It was just an intellectual fad. We used to meet in somebody's attic in graduate school (I was thirty, L. B. was thirty-five) until a media rep got hold of it and then all of a sudden there were neo-Christians everywhere, like Amanita mushrooms. That's when I quit. Who wants to sit in an attic and argue about Descartes, anyway? It was only stealing ideas, but I suppose it'll go into the history books as 'eclectic.'

History is all fantasy.

It's boring. Starving is boring. I just went over everything I dictated to the vocoder, then decided to leave it as it was. What's the use of listening? All you hear is your own voice. I ought to rig up the machine to wake me in the middle of the night and whisper something shocking like, 'We're going to get you!' In my voice, of course. Would if I had the tools.

I certainly have the time.

It is so boring that I am here and now going to write the history of the neo-Christian movement, which began with a classmate of mine named L. B. Hook (he played the tuba) and ended in spectacular persecutions, martyrs who shrieked their faith aloud in the flames, no no, we never got the chance, worse luck. It ended like everything else, just sort of petered out. Like dyeing your eyelashes a different color every week or regulating all your daily movements with a pocket watch according to the Leuter system of exercises. Other hobbies. Mixed with Zen, old Christianity, vegetarianism, archery, astrology, don't know what. Whatever.

No, I won't write it. No reason to. I'm sure that − presenting no threat to the Powers That Be − it's amply documented somewhere. (Actually I did talk out a long history of the whole business and then erased it. It took up perhaps half an hour. Passed the time. I can't tell now the difference between my politics at the time and my love affairs, between music and economics, or economics and metaphysics. I was drunk when L. B. and I went to the jeweler's to get our crosses made, you know, one of those little places that always exists: planting the flag of handmade pottery everywhere! The neo-Christian symbol was a cross inside a circle − that is, a quartered circle − which probably comes from some other iconography, but we always called it a cross. Had an awful time making the man understand what we wanted. I kept mine in memory of L. B. and getting drunk.

(And my attempting − drunk − to play the tuba.)

*

Dull. Oh God, dull. Trying hopelessly to push the sun along. If you scream, will that move it? I can't get through the next minute, I know I can't. Count your fingers one way and then back (nineteen), assigning them metaphysical values or pictures: house, book, Byzantine Empire, salvation, orthodoxy, burnt bacon, play, and so on. Do it backwards; can you remember them? Clock watching. Sun watching. The sun doesn't set directly in back of the cave but almost downstream. That's why I can see it rise.

I think the rising place and the setting place are moving closer together.

If it moves over *that bush*, I'll survive. If it hits the edge of *that tree*, I'll stay sane. Then I can leave work and go home. Block out the disc with one palm and count: seventy-five pulse beats for the bush, a hundred and fifty for the tree. If I didn't move my head or my hand or my arm and didn't get excited. I marked out elaborate divisions on the sun-dial, scratching them in the dirt, then threw the biggest rocks to the side of the cave. Much tidier. Thought I'd save the rest of them so it would leave me something to do, then with an absurd sense of utter defeat, sat down and cried.

I'm not afraid of death but there's nothing to do. Nothing, nothing, nothing.

I wept.

Had a brilliant idea: to recite all the poetry and prose I ever remembered into the vocoder, have it print-out. I'll have a library.

Didn't do it.

Sat and sat. Stopped being hungry for a while. I feel all right except that it's odd to swallow water as if it were food and feel that everything's *cleared up*, somehow, not that anything's happened to my vision. There used to be bulk cellulose you could buy for starving, i.e. dieting, but there's nothing to buy here. The withdrawal symptoms of a buying addict. A talking addict. A busy-ness addict. The sun says: Sloooooow Dooooooown.

Well, maybe (have to do something special to the vocoder to get it to do that, above).

If:

beef teriyaki
caramel sauce
vanilla cream
frenchfries
noodles with pork
bombe glacée
pressed seaweed sticks
Salt!
I forgot salt; I'm going to die for lack of salt.

A false alarm, of course. But I gave myself a jolt of adrenalin that –
you know – crying, trembling a lot, walking around, wringing
the hands – I do carry salt with me, for there are places where it's
very expensive, not a drug but terrestrial sea-salt for gourmets.
And there's more back at the bungalow. There's food back there.

That frightened me. Made me hungry for food, even though
there are corpses back there. And hungry for the company back
there, too. (That's not exactly clear-headed.) I spread out everything I owned, pop-outs from my belt, stuff in the jacket, in my
shoe-heels, et cetera, and marked in my mind what and where,
and then put it back. Must not, should not, cannot take off anything for a moment. Must be with me, always. Wished I had the
broom. Still, I could walk it. Must've spent about ten minutes taking all those drugs out and putting them back again but I couldn't
even get up; I was trembling. Heart pounding. Very dizzy.

Did I put a pebble down? Can't remember. I put another, which
made four. Five. Six. Seven. Eight. Nine. Ten. Eleven. Twelve. I
don't think you can die from lack of salt all that fast. Looked very
nice. I made a circle of them, then scrambled them up, then scrab-
bled about for a whole bunch of pebbles and made on the floor – by
laying them out neatly and carefully – the picture of the quartered
circle.

Too late for exploring. That was the idea: no food, no broomstick. You're not supposed to change your mind. If I lie still for a
few minutes my head clears and I can talk connectedly, e.g. there's

something trying to get into this cave or into my head. No, not for real. But something.

Going to sleep now. Nothing will change.

Next day, don't know what day it is. Probably five. Who cares. If history were not fantasy, then one could ask to be remembered but history is fake and memories die when you do and only God (don't believe it) remembers. History always rewritten. Nobody will find this anyway or they'll have flippers so who cares.

Sign off.

Late afternoon: these were my politics: Communism and share-the-work. If you can't tell Communism from Socialism, Socialism from Anarchism, go away. The theory: a new class, even a new economy, developing within our mimicry of the old one, big business, big government, big labor, and all science, and out of it comes the real producers. A short chain formed from part of a long chain that's doubled back on itself. Look carefully or you won't see that much government is little government, much business little business, most labor little labor, but all science big science. Now.

The truth is, they don't need us.

Will we be killed off eventually as simply unnecessary? Or kept as house pets?

(Questions: What is 'house pets.' What is 'eventually.' What is 'politics.' What is 'Communism.' What is 'economy.' What is 'mimicry.' What is 'labor.' What is 'business.' What is 'doubled.' What is 'theory.' What is 'class.' What is 'Anarchism.' What is 'Socialism.' What is 'producers.'

(If you and your flippers get that far.)

Vocoder has made eighteen spaces, which I erased. If neither alien nor human, you're God. Who already knows. So I'm left talking to myself. Which is nothing and nobody.

⋆

I guess I'd better tell you about my politics because you're such nice people you might think I did something wrong but I didn't. I got into the Populars at about age twenty-six and spent about a year talking to University groups and various funded groups (these are the most vulnerable because the most parasitic) until in some inexplicable way the tide turned against us (although the media had never picked us up) and one night I heard a sound from the audience that doesn't need explaining any more than the shape of a chicken-hawk to a chicken, something I can only describe as a growing volume in the infra-bass as if the floor were preparing to rise and the walls come tumbling down, an ominous, slowly-rising roar that has nothing whatsoever to do with shouting or heckling; they're nothing. I stood listening to that fascinating sound until it occurred to me that they were after me — me, who had never harmed them! — and then I ran. I sprinted into the wings, smiled charmingly at the Fund officials (who were trying to grab me), twisted the pinky finger of one lady, stepped hard on the bare instep of another gentleman (but smiling, smiling all the time), dropped my over-tunic in the hall (bright red-and-green, far too distinctive) and took the fire-elevator to the third sub-basement, thus avoiding a long discussion with the fire marshals in the lobby in which you have to say for five minutes Gee, I'm sorry, I didn't know I wasn't supposed to do that (then you show them your ID), found the freight elevators locked, and finally staggered up three staircases, took an ordinary elevator to the street level, and walked inconspicuously out of the building. Don't know where all those sudden skills came from. It was fun in a way. But not the kind of thing you'd want to do twice.

I didn't even go home for two days but when I did, nothing happened.

Oh the jail, that was later, that was a lark. Four neo-Christians talking to some incredible aardvark like a real, live Civic Improvement Association in a city park during a summer windstorm that backed up a small, ornamental lake and flooded the place. We were rather perfunctorily arrested and locked in the storage shed used for the carousel in wintertime. Place damp and full of old picnic tables, which we sat on. And sang. And played dominoes. And took bets if the water would rise enough to float us away. I had to keep my feet on the tables because I was the only one wearing shoes and when the friendly police couple let us out to run to the public bathroom (ten meters away) I remember taking them off (the shoes) and leaving them on a table. Nobody touched them.

I've told this story a hundred times and people are always impressed and I am damned if I know why.

That enormous building I spoke in (or almost got killed in): the interior carpet-sprayed and wall-flocked in a certain extremely limited range of bright, stylized colors, everything flat and dry to the touch, neither cold nor hot, and you can't smell anything except the carpets (if they're new) or maybe the disinfectants blown through the air ducts at night. Brochures often describe the hologrammic numerals hanging in front of the doors in such buildings as 'softly glowing' – which means they're in the same range of colors as everything else but the hall is dimmed a little so you can see them and they carry the intangibleness and non-tactility of the place to the point of driving you gaga. Books say it. Actors on TV say it. Everyone says it except people.

Yet the style of architecture is a good eighty years old. We are trapped in somebody's old dreams of Utopia, trapped outside what's really new. Modern Baroque is new: think of those non-civilian buildings we know about: great, opal-streaked globes, each with its separate stem, those sixty-four-square chessboards you find in Iowa, each grid half a mile on a side, spaghetti-clusters of transparent tubing for private homes or the same stuff, twenty times as big, built over rivers or waterfalls for factories. Nobody keeps us out. Nobody forbids us. You can even go in and get yourself a tour – only you'll never learn enough to go home and reproduce it yourself. If you had the tools. Which you don't.

My God, how naive we were. If somebody tried to bust us up, we must've been going in the right direction. I mean the Pops, the Pops, of course, not the other – and I knew it. (And the media never even touching us!)

Although the Civic Improvement Association was worse (or better?); anyway, they still thought they were *at the center*. You have to think that or die. Either you limit what you think about and who you think about (the commonest method) or you start raising a ruckus about being outside and wanting to get inside (then they try to kill you) or you say piously that God puts everybody on the inside (then they love you) or you become crazed in some way. Not insane but flawed deep down somehow, like a badly-fired pot that breaks when you take it out of the kiln and the cold air hits it. Desperate.

So I said Hey, if you're going to send mobs against me, I'll change what I say; I'll say God puts everybody on the inside – and anyway it's true and one must believe it – and I zipped like lightning back to the edge of the board. The music (which I like) and the audiences (which I don't) and the catching cold (run out of Interferogen) and the too-much-reading when I travel (because I'm bored) and the paid corps of nitwits who travel one day ahead of me so they can ask the identical, stupid questions over and over, meanwhile (in between lectures) frantically changing their height, their weight, their coloring, their faces, and their voices – everything but their minds.

Far, far away from the cutting edge of change.

God knows I'm private now. And on the periphery now. As far from anything as one can get. Outside the outside of the outside.

I dozed and dreamed. Thought I'd got my period. But I seem to have gone anestrous, way off my regular schedule. First time in my life. I guess I'm already too skinny; I'll be amenorrheic forever.

A cheap vocoder could not spell that: 'amenorrheic.'

I've thought this through a hundred times; was going to erase it. Didn't, though.

The sun's moved.

A blessing.

★

83

Morning. Dreamed near waking, something very confused and vivid. It was about catching cold, but I don't remember what the cold was supposed to be. Ears ringing with solitude. It's so quiet that I seem to be at the center of a noise-factory: gurgling innards, bellows in my chest, all sorts of scraping and scratching of skin against clothes or pebbles moving. Even one knee that clicks, I swear.

It's hotter. Though I should be putting out less heat because of not eating. There was a thermometer back in the bungalow.

No. Sit still.

The old monks: 'Sit in thy cell and thy cell will teach thee all things.' Helps if you've got a cell in the middle of downtown San Francisco.

I feel a reluctance to speak into this machine. Because something is leaning over my shoulder. Is in here with me now. Is at the door. Is coming in. Is outside the cave. Which probably means I'm starting to go bananas.

Rest. For a while.

Well, I still can't think of death properly, can I, though I worked for more than a year in the terminal counseling end of a hospital in San Francisco. I mean death is what happens *in a hospital*, nobody just dies, for goodness' sakes, and if you want death there's no sense getting ready for it anywhere else than a hospital because you won't get it. You have to order it, like a special diet. And pray for it. And take medication for it. And consult with your doctors about it. And be in a hospital bed. Which is nonsense.

Wish I'd gotten rid of the food back at the bungalow.

(I tried to get up and my head swam; everything whirled.)

Anyway it's not so bad because the worst kind I ever saw were those whose lives had gone long before their bodies. The useless people. Screaming, 'I don't want to die, I don't want to die!' the way children still scream at the allergist's, sometimes, having whispered to each other long, ancient, horror stories about 'needles' (allergists don't use them). Clinging to money and power

84

because there's nothing else. (A five-year-old boy screaming himself blue in the Allergy Room with everyone standing patiently at least two meters from him. He had shut his eyes in convulsive stubbornness; then I saw a doctor say, 'All right, Stevie, we won't do it,' and give him the shot. Opened his eyes and cried, 'All right. Do it! Do it now!') The number of old hands I've held, saying: Dying is a task. (One wit answered, 'Come and join me, then.')

Hello. Hello, old wit.

It never moves in stranger ways than when It moves inside us.

There'll be hallucinations about being rescued, I know: croaking thinly, 'no, let me die!' (with immense dignity, of course) and I'm carried out to a shuttlecraft by great, coarse, strong, disgustingly healthy people in uniforms, with thick necks. Actually it would be a little awkward trying to explain what happened to the others.

You killed them. Why?

They were trying to kill me.

Why?

To prevent me.

From doing what?

Dying.

A shadow at the mouth of the cave. Wasn't. My mistake. I can't have gone hungry that long, it's only a few days; must be spooking myself.

Sleep some more.

I know, I know, I'm an awful stupe. We all knew, really. If the media ignored something as big as the Pops (and other such, as I found out later), it wasn't because we were dull; it's because we were dangerous. They would have publicized a miniature Sheboygan World Trade Tower made out of waffles and they did. Mind you, there doesn't have to be that much of a conspiracy if your social reflexes are automatic enough. Then I asked a friend to drift past the building where I'd (not) spoken and she said there was God's own amount of repair material going up to the forty-third floor: women with carpet-sprayers' guns, men with the other rig for the walls, bales of sheet plastic that you use to cover things you don't want colored, plyboard, furniture, even packages of searchlight lenses flown down on to the roof. My, my, my! And not a word of it anywhere. Now that's real censorship.

That's when I cut out. With no qualms.

I know, religion vs. politics (q.v.) the whole bit: saving people retail is OK but don't do it wholesale. My one original contribution to the whole business was a graffito that nobody would use although I thought it rather zippy myself: *'Money doesn't matter when/Control is somewhere else!'* (Although I saw it in the Auckland underground station years later so maybe it got somewhere. Or occurred to someone else, which isn't unlikely.)

I knew all those things. But never in my life did I make such an absolute, inflexible, and somehow automatic decision. And I stuck to it even though it wasn't (in some curious way) mine at all. I wasn't angry. I wasn't even afraid. I was, in fact, in some odd way, rather pleased with myself. I knew, of course, that the tide turning against us wasn't 'inexplicable' but I didn't care as the others did; I only wondered how they did it, exactly. And who 'they' were. And admired them. And thought I'd like to meet them, if I could, and find out what they were really up to.

Never will, of course.

And what will neo-Christianity do in the future? Will it mean anything? That does bother me.

It's a bore, a dreadful bore, being outside history.

Day something. Dreams about Cassie. I woke up and actually saw her stand at the door of the cave. Then she vanished; I mean became again the patterns of rock and sun-spots-in-my-eyes I'd been making her out of. Hallucinations aren't just 'seeing something'; they're a special case of perception in which you work a little harder, that's all.

Cassie. Every mind is its own galaxy. If I told Cassie I had wanted to be inside History, she'd say, 'Oh, so you want to be *important*, do you?' I'm an awful snob. I must move around. Only starve to death a little sooner, that's all, but this sedentariness is enough to make you sick by itself. For a moment I had a violent craving for the broomstick, anything, car, helicopter, GEV, monorail, anything that lets you move, move, move. I'll go out; breaking a leg doesn't matter because it'll just speed things up. I can go out on my own front porch anyway, I should hope to kiss a pig. If I hold on to the wall.

Cassie. Go. Away. Please?

I'll be seeing her all day now, in flashes, out of the corner of my eye.

She's very polite. She went away.

I know you are wondering by now how I can do so much and keep talking all the time; what I have done is to tie a strip of cloth through the hook on the vocoder and hang the vocoder around my neck. It goes with me. So I will go out on the cave porch with it, and sit on the edge of the ledge and get the giggles about falling. This is it:

There is a low and impossible sun in the painted backdrop of the sky. So bleak. So empty. Might as well be unreal if I can't get into it. The color is as strange as anything I've ever seen, though part of that must be the light: pale, Northern sunlight that slides down these equivocal stems or what aren't really bushes – or trees – and ought to be somewhere in Death Valley National Park anyway, not within the Arctic Circle. River-noise is clear now (somebody behind the scenes just turned up a switch and thank you very much).

I like this place. It's nice.

I know Cassie is an hallucination because she doesn't move, just appears for an instant in that attitude in which I saw her last (arms and legs sprawled, staring straight up) but she appears vertically instead of horizontally because that's how she was in my field of vision then because I was looking at her from above. She's like a portable cut-out.

Hallucinations can be memories, too. If I tried I could hear in the noise of the river the sound of the rain on the old carousel shed in the park; I could invent the sound of a door slamming shut somewhere from time to time, irregularly, as the wind whipped about. (I tried to drink from out of an unboarded window and got my shoes wet in the puddle that'd blown in under it.) Or the sound of the audience that was going to kill me – you can't get that from actors, you know; it's inimitable – that one's easy if you start with the noise of river-water. Something very similar about the echoes, the undertones, the simultaneity of sources. I remember quite vividly standing on the platform and being able to see nothing but the light cage in the back of the hall, wondering if the bored-looking person in it would turn the lights off me and on to the audience because if you do that they can sometimes be diverted into smashing the lights, at least for a while. But I guess she was paid not to. (Though they broke a lot of glassware anyway; at least the lenses were being replaced wholesale a day later.) I said, smiling, 'I'm not the speaker' – or at least I became aware that I was in the middle of saying it – and then the floor of the room started to rise with the sheer volume of the sound and I walked off.

Don't know what happened to my friends.

Did the Pops start as three people in an attic? By the time it got to us it was a traveling symposium, which shows you it was past that stage or maybe was never in it, though some of the speakers were – God knows – bad enough to be idealistic amateurs.

Another graffito: '*I have just lost all my fingers to/The cutting edge of change.*'

I must've been the smallest minnow ever to slip through that kind of a net. If there was a net. When there's no real organization you don't need to catch anybody; just scare them sufficiently and the whole thing dissolves back into individuals.

No, Cassie. No. No. No. Go away.

She moved. She'll be talking next.

Thought I'd go down to the bungalow – surely I could find my way there and back, just follow the river – but I don't walk very well. It's a long way up to get up. Or something. Anyway, I got hideously lightheaded, probably from having spent so much time sitting down. I will probably get scurvy or an ulcer. Cassie and I had a long talk (which I know is imaginary).

I don't remember a thing about it

Things are for the best and if they aren't I certainly am not going to make a fuss about it. Not now. Like the time I was under anesthesia for a tooth implant and kept murmuring dreamily to myself, 'I don't care what you do to *Me* so long as I am not here.' (Which came out, they tell me, as something like 'ff . . . ff . . . ff . . . ') It was such a relief. Then you come to, spitting blood and sick to your stomach.

Guess I really am starving. But not apathetic enough (yet) to stop talking. Never will, I guess. Everything's being sublimed into voice, sacrificed for voice; my voice will live on years and years after I die, thus proving that the rest of me was faintly comic at best, perhaps impossible, just an organic backup for conversation. Marvelous, marvelous conversation! The end of life.

And music's coming back. Bits of Handel this morning, swaying in the pine trees. I mean in memory, of course, I'm not that cracked.

Not yet.

My father dying in a hospital, years ago, under the loose, transparent folds of an oxygen tent, weakly grabbing my hand: 'I don't want to die!' I said, 'You won't.' (An oxygen tube taped to his nose.)

But he knew.

There's a neo-Christian exercise for this sort of thing, which you are supposed to prepare for by taking a good stiff jog around the block, which under the circumstances is, I think, just a little bit impractical.

Must be some other ones.

I drink when I'm thirsty; when I'm tired I sleep. Everything's so close together here. I stand up and wait until my head clears, then straddle this hygienic little streamlet. Brilliant possibility: sitting in it and let the bladder go. A sort of ambulating bedpan, and without the usual plumber's attachment, too. It's warm enough to go naked. A scientist might be able to make up theories about this cave, but I can only look at it. Which I do, during breathing exercises (told you there were other ones). I've been standing up more — starving is overrated, doesn't get you that fast — and then a walk round the cave, then a rest, then two more walks. I am sitting cross-legged, talking this. There's no reason to collapse if you don't collapse. If I fell over the edge I'd even be able to get back (in an hour or so) so why not. Putting my legs over the edge of the ledge and hooting. Although the bungalow's certainly too far and I bet that food's rotten by now.

Why didn't I bring a mirror with me? Clever, perhaps, not to; I could hang it on some projection of rock or branch, let my face go into it, my identity, and be faceless forever more. And there's nothing to blow my nose in (except my fingers) because I can't catch cold, nobody to catch it from.

Starving doesn't drive you mad. But solitude does.

Morning. A morning. Studied the rock wall of the cave, extraordinarily beautiful and rich, such full arrangements of color and shape, such extremely crowded information. Fra Angelico painted on his knees. I really couldn't get over the textures (perception is abstraction), how little detail it takes to see them (though perhaps it's half memory), how they fit so. But then of course everything fits; it has to, if it didn't fit it couldn't exist, not on this world or any other. I fell to sniffling a little. Then I stopped because crying usually puts an end to this and if things got very good, maybe I could make the people come back: the edge of a naked plant-root, taking a shortcut for a moment out of the wall and haloed by the sun in all its little hairs, wet pebbles shining at the back of the cave where the stream comes through, rocks loudly declaring their own internal structure by their shape, by their color, by the places where they broke, and everything mutely going hallelujah on the gravity of transcendent gravity: the earth and rubbish piled up against it, the water dropping down with it, occasionally wobbling a stick (more gravity) or prying loose a few darkish grains of something. The eloquence of it. The mutual agreement of it. What to do if the elements fall to quarreling? I knew if I cried it would stop so I didn't. I just waited.

It went away.

(Thinking sentimentally: Sit in thy cell and thy cell will teach thee all things.)

Outside was afternoon. The round planet turning into the cone of its own shadow. A youth in the something of his something lying. (Can't remember.) This endless whirling that is taking us noplace, so you think they'd stop.

I wanted to stay up and watch the night sky but began to doze a bit on the ledge so I went back in. I guess the habits of sleeping were too strong.

So this should be not morning but the next morning. If I did part of it then. Must have because I say I went to sleep in the late afternoon and I remember that I did. But I can't find the break in the tape.

So dating things is no use.

Cassie. The only one I liked. The gossip we could have had. Even behind the mask of John Ude must have been something human, though if you will pardon my cynicism I doubt it, having had far too much to do with that type before.

But Cassie . . . !

The point is, when I cross over, will I meet only Victor? And do people who have died naturally, as we call it, go somewhere different or cross over in some different way than those who have died by violence? This is physically and metaphysically silly, the whole damned subject, but it does seem to have preoccupied people: different heavens in Scandinavian mythology, different hells in Dante, no heaven at all for the Greeks. Ghosts stuck in the place where they got strangled and so forth.

If those seven and I ever get together; the only thing they'll want to do to me will be kill me, and that will be rather difficult under the circumstances.

Eternity with Victor: could do worse.

But Cassie . . . I know I'm romanticizing something about my own life, or something that isn't in my own life. We always make such distinctions between those of us who are us and those of us who are tables and chairs and then some table turns up and *thinks* at you, criticizes you, talks to you, looks down on you.

Likes you.

Little twelve-year-old girls walking about with billions of dollars of improvements inside them. Like dolls with tape-decks in a slot in the back.

Not that she felt that way, of course.

What were the Grahams like at home? An 'At-Home,' that is. Mr and Mrs Graham at home Tuesday next. But where? High, high up on Staten Island with a real, polarized city window from which you can see all the other private millionaires' spires and perhaps even the river? No, too small. They'd have an estate pitched on the ruins of what used to be Adirondack cattle country (with the farmland underneath now, not above) or way up in Northern Maine where nobody ever went anyhow, a real, honest-to-God estate with piles sunk into the marsh and a heli field. (New-money faddy, old-money relaxed. Some of each.) Royal-blue curtains over glass that doesn't always reveal the Maine tundra (that's old-money) but that doesn't always substitute some other three-dimensional scene either (too vulgar). Forty years of gold and royal blue, everything that Valeria wants and yet Victor's rather proud of himself, really (especially when he reaches the age at which she has to pay him and can take it easy), fond of his wife but absolutely crazy about Lori. Reverting to type. I think Val first chose royal blue to flatter herself and then dyed her hair to flatter the royal blue, stuck in it, so to speak, liking it. The eyes of the old are blue-hungry.

Alan-Bobby, totally harmless in most places to most people.

Even, I suspect, running earnestly about the field, panting while solemnly playing *le futbol*.

And Sister Nathalie. Mirror-sister Nathalie. That vicious woman. I almost said to her once, aboard ship, 'Wait a few years; you won't be so eager.' But she was, desperate with her unbearable hatred of civilians, barely able to control herself until she could pass over into that other, real world.

What would she have done if there'd been no accident? If she'd got there – and trained – and flunked?

Become a music lecturer. Of course.

Cassie, Cassie, come out to play.

Come over for a chat.

I don't mind if you're rotting.

I stayed up last night to see The Smudge and locate sunrise, which is distinctly closer to sunset than it was. Plan: to kill myself on the exact, glorious day of the summer solstice but I won't know what day that is until several days afterward. Which makes things difficult. (Like the old recipe for nitroglycerine: stop heating one second before it explodes.)

There was a streak of light at the zenith, falling towards the Poleward horizon, looking mighty like a Patrol ship coming in for a landing but much too fast.

Then another.

And another. All over the sky. A meteor swarm. As if veils were being plucked off the stars moment by moment and they'd been there all along. I watched until we rotated out of whatever debris it was, then marked where the sun came up (my position, nose on ground, where my feet were and where – from that – the sun was behind the sundial). Then I slept. I dreamed that a ship landed somewhere and sent a party that tried to rescue me, me with cunning patience hiding in my cave and shooting down every single one of them. Woke up with some long and involved declaration – myself or person or persons unknown – fading in my hearing. It came back only when I lay down again, just before I drifted off, i.e.:

No use trying to rescue that one; can't you tell a corpse when you see it?
(I am elegantly self-satisfied. My fakery is working.)
She's been walking around dead for years.

Evening. Dawn. Morning? Can't tell.

I started to say something.

★ ★ ★

Oh yes. It's hotter. I feel fine. I've been sitting with my feet in the stream – mustn't sit right in it or it backs up over everything – and I can move well enough if I keep it slow. Or lying on my stomach, playing with the water. Obese people in clinics can starve painlessly for months and what do they have that I don't have except some idiot in a pale-blue (ill-fitting) coat who comes around every morning and says 'Aha!' (?) Only I'm not obese. Only I haven't gotten any skinnier. Only I haven't looked because I don't want to know and I'm not going to, either.

　　Whoever you
　　Whoever finds

Cassie's come. Doesn't do anything, just sits against the wall (my favorite wall, too! the other's got big boulders sticking out of it) with her arms folded and looks at me. I've put the vocoder on whisper so she won't hear. Not that I expect she's real; if I got up she'd probably rise in my field of vision like all hallucinations do – either stand up or float in the air – I have a talent for these things, always did; had to be careful with all those neo-Christian 'exercises.' Could never be hypnotized without drugs, though, probably a defense against my own imagination.

　　I said to her (smugly, I'm afraid), 'I can't be hypnotized.'

　　Words in my mind: *You're schizoid.*

　　Insults! Insults from her.

94

We had a long — no, we didn't; that's an invention; I simply could not help looking at her because when you hallucinate or remember, that is your center of energy, I mean you're creating it. So you get fixed on it. And I watched her. Breathless. Not frightened. In suspense.

She did nothing.

I'll tell you how she went away; this isn't really visual, you see, it's a matter of conviction and what happened was the conviction went out of me and I knew I was looking at a memory. There was a pattern of roots and shadows and a ghost and a pattern of roots and shadows and a ghost. Then the memory goes. Nothing positive but it's not there and *of course* she picked that side — it's all rocks and shadows.

When they finally arrive, what will they all say to me?

I was very cross with her.

Day again. There's a philosophical problem here. Falling asleep, waking, hard or soft, hunger, eating, illness, feeling sex, running, being dizzy — why can't we remember them? They evaporate. Right now I can't remember a hot bath. About my tooth implant, I remember the office, the medical lady in the pale-green coat, what everyone said, what I thought under the anesthetic, and the extreme oddity of it, too, I remember that. But I can't remember the pain. There's only a warning muddle somewhere at the back of the experience, a faint haze of obfuscation. Now I know that physiologically, literally, it's still all there — all in my brain waiting to be waked up. I mean if you had the proper electrodes. But why can't I wake it up, dammit? The second time I had a tooth put in I didn't remember but my feet knew (they kept trying to turn around and walk me out of the office) and I suppose my body knew (I couldn't sleep the night before) but I didn't know. Until it began to happen again and then I wondered: how could I ever forget!

And then I forgot.

You know, I was very old-fashioned as a teenager; I really

thought that a real physical letting-go (pleasure, anger, anything where I'd stop controlling myself – I called it 'stop thinking') would absolutely bring the roof down around my ears, or if it didn't lead to instant death, disgrace, shatterment, and horror, it would cure me right away of all my 'problems' and I would never be unhappy again. Don't know where this came from; it must have been in the air because nobody ever told me in so many words, but we are still – maybe it's the price we pay for being so rich – a Puritanical people.

I was *so* disappointed!

Primary things – the stuff bodily experience is made of – just don't last.

Even music, beautiful music, hearing that won't last unless you translate it into ideas, put it into your head, recreate it, drum it in. A weird business: grief without bodily pain, joy without bodily pleasure, emotion without flesh, idea-joy, idea-grief, but it makes you shiver and it makes you cry and it can be dreadful and wonderful and unbearable. And that's not the body making you feel (which of course it can); it's the body trying only to follow what you feel. To mean, not be. Which the body is not good at.

(For example, fucking. Why is it sometimes rememberable and sometimes not. And what do you remember? I think either a picture or an emotion but not the physical thing itself, not half an hour later, sometimes. Like a dried leaf. A dead rose. A taste that's gone. Actors practice sensory memory for years and even they have to turn it into something else. I mean put it into their heads, translate it into ideas.

(I can so vividly recall Marilyn, who must have drifted past that eighty-story building with terrific aplomb – as always – with her hands in her pockets – saying to me quietly, 'it's not in the papers' right after 'they're rebuilding the whole floor' with her usual, slightly hesitant way of speaking, as if she were apologizing for the triviality of what she was saying and yet always very passionate about it, and wrinkling her forehead in anxiety above those queer, huge, round, owl-like eyeglasses she always wore, looking at me with her magnified eyes as if to say: now we both know. And also: the world is falling apart.

(I also remember L. B. trying to get a contra-tuba – of all things – through the door of the attic where we were holding a neo-Christian meeting and not quite succeeding and finally sitting on the landing outside that very expensive attic, which was in a house made of real, restored wood (practically a national monument) with his large, delicate, slightly flushed ears sticking out – as always – and finally managing on that absurd, coiled, huge instrument to produce a dreadful, toneless, melancholy howl like that of a locomotive *in extremis*, as if the last nineteenth-century steam engine in the Smithsonian were finally expiring and telling everybody about it.

(I remember the third time we made love and how I decided it must be so very different because the room was different or I was just precisely drunk enough – though I wasn't drunk at all – or had eaten for once exactly the proper kind of dinner. He said it was because we had the contra-tuba in the room with us and that the contra-tuba, alone among all the instruments of the orchestra, had a soul. My memory of him is built up of many, many times after this, all made into one, just like the year I was speaking for the Populars and in just the same way: an intelligent, ruthless abstraction of *what mattered*, details plucked unhesitatingly from the real, unstable times and places and put together into a meaning, a mosaic, a symbol, an icon, because that's what mattered and that's how it mattered, and because I knew more than I ever have before or since just what mattered and what that meaning was.

(Meaning preserves things by isolating them, by taking them beyond themselves, making them transcendent, revealing their real insides by pointing beyond them.

(If we perceived everything, we would know nothing. There would be no pattern.

(But I don't remember hunger. I chose that because it fits intellectually. I don't feel it. Though I recall very clearly my rage when I was seven and told to eat my loathesome soup because little

97

children were starving in . . . well, you pick a place. Alone in my gleeful rage among eleven well-behaved little boys and girls, it was I who pushed forward my bowl and said, in sly satisfaction, 'Send it to them.' How do you ship soup? When I was six there was the first real space travel, I mean instantaneously from one point to another; I remember this only because the whole topic was so profoundly uninteresting and we all had to sit still to hear about it. And I remember — at ten — remembering what a nump I'd been at six and wishing I had remembered all the right, glorious, proper, great things about that great day instead of the silly damn-fool things I did remember: that Ruby Fossett beat up Charlie Washington for saying black people were the same as Indians and Indians had to come from India, so black people couldn't have come from Africa; that somebody called somebody else Slotface and knocked over my block bridge (accidentally); that at dinner I gave some vegetables I didn't like to Ruby Fossett who got rid of them in some awesome and mysterious way without eating them. But I knew Ruby Fossett was a magical person because she was seven and could stand on her head and had a big, beautiful, rusty-red 'fro, which was by far the most impressive hair I had ever seen. I do not, by the way, remember what the Day-care answered when I offered my slopping soup to be mailed to the starving children; I think he just imitated the Great Stone Face. Don't really remember Charlie's last name, either; it was something else, I think. And I don't remember what the Center looked like, even. I don't remember much.

(And Hunger's gone. Kachina-mask-dancing Hunger like a figure in a play, that I can imagine. Or a word in a dictionary with pronunciation marks over it. Or I hunger for righteousness, that's a metaphor. But I cannot even begin to imagine what I felt. Or that I felt at all; it's dropped out of the world. It's a hole. It's nothing.

(Not even nothing. Just the intellectual conviction that there ought to be a gap somewhere. Only that.)

So ideas stick. Meanings stick. Anything you can force inside your head and keep it there. Also emotion. Which shouldn't last but it does. My God, it lasts and lasts. Wish it didn't.

Old poem: when the bones are clean and the dead bones gone . . . but I'm getting it wrong. The Celts had three lasting things: Grass and Copper and Yew. The Germans had something else, some other story. Medieval Europe seems to have valorized such games: this number of lasting things, that number of changing things, so many wonderful things, so many sins, so many virtues.

I have Six Lasting Things: Valeria, Nathalie, Cassandra, John, Alan, and Lori.

Especially Lori.

There was a trial. Dreams merging into wakefulness, back to dreams again. I was very cross. They ranged themselves round the cave, knowing I was too weak, too tired, too starved, to get away. It wasn't fair. Big, dark shapes I couldn't see. When you first wake up you can't see clearly and everything's flat; that's when a coat hanging on a closet door becomes something huge standing over you, until you can see in depth again. It's the closeness that's threatening, right on your eyeballs. Things at the foot of the bed or right on the bed, but it's really a picture on the wall or a window curtain. When I'm badly off. When I'm tired. I couldn't see their faces. I sat up and thought I would go to the water purifier to wash my face but I couldn't. I was too tired. I lay down again – or stood up, I can't remember – anyway it was none of their business and I hadn't invited them.

I said, 'Go away.'

They just shifted a little.

John Ude said . . .

Then Nathalie said . . . and Cassandra said . . . and Alan said . . .

Then John Ude said again . . .

I yelled, 'You're always first, aren't you? You and the goddamn government! I bet you were a clerk. I bet you never got within five miles of anything real.'

He said, *You know that I worked for the real government.*

'You are a damned, damned bully,' I told him; 'But who can you bully now? Who are you going to bully through eternity?'

You.

Silence.

I said, 'All right, I'm a coward. Satisfied? I didn't have the guts to stand up against you in '25; I let myself be scared off. But what does it matter now? We're all here now, aren't we? And there'll be others. And my religion is just as real and just as important as the other so don't you go tampering with that. Don't you go telling me I'm an escapist or something.'

He said, *God is easier than guns.*

Silence. I don't believe him. It's just what he'd say. You can shoot a lot of things but you can't shoot down death. And if you capture a tank, what can you use it for except what a tank does? You can't plant a garden with it.

Coward, he said.

I said, 'Oh go to hell.' (Quickly, as if it were one word, the way you do. You know.)

Killer coward. But it was a worse word than that, somehow, I don't know what it was, and not John Ude who is only a mask. I looked at the people standing around my home, dressed as I had seen them last and with not a mark of death on them; there's no fogginess in this cave. It is from the big boulder on the left-hand side as you face out – counting clockwise – John, every inch The Professor, polishing his pipe on the edge of his (now rather ragged) jacket; Cassandra (who looks away from me, head averted as if she didn't want to talk to me in her white sheet or was ashamed or disliked me); and then Valeria, who stands with her arms clasped in front of her loosely but looking very severe; and beyond her (on the other side, none of them are standing in the sunlight) Nathalie – again separated from them all – disgusted, fiercely impatient with everyone, sitting with her knees under her chin, scowling and pitching pebbles at the cave floor. Then Lori, who's reading a big, illustrated storybook with a fairy-tale cover, a fairy godmother or something like that, and beyond her in the shadows, but somehow luminous, young, and very beautiful, standing with his arms folded across his chest, emotionless now, the one who called me a killer.

Killer coward, said Alan-Bobby for the second time.

I said, 'I suppose you're in on this little kangaroo-court because I wasn't stuck on you, like Lori, and you didn't get to beat me up, like Nathalie, and I didn't praise the shit out of you, like the men, so I guess I just didn't kowtow enough to your beautiful, strong, masculine bod, huh?'

He said, *I had none.*

Silence.

I had the muscles of an ox, which always embarrassed me, I was not beautiful, I was stupid, and I knew nothing.

That's Alan-Bobby now, who is thinking or talking or somehow putting these words into my mind, standing angelically tall in the darkness of the cave (which should be too low for him; that's how he bashed his head) and somehow lighting himself up from inside, like a Christmas-tree candle. He is so lovely. He said:

We're dead. So we're wise. But still, you killed me. Is it allowed to kill fools?

You killed me, said Lori, uninterested, glancing up for a moment from her book.

And me, said Valeria with calm evenness, and I saw with surprise – no, really with astonishment – that although she could have – well, I suppose, being dead, you know – I mean she could have come back in her blue-and-gold Indian sari, her gold jewelry, anything she liked, but she hadn't. She was in trousers and blouse, just the way I'd last seen her. Her hair was grey at the roots.

She said, *You killed me. I was half-crazy then. Is it permitted to kill the crazy or the rich? Is it permitted to kill someone weak and old whom you could have disarmed?*

And me, said John Ude urbanely, pulling on his unlit pipe. *A reasonable man who could have been persuaded, a despairing man whose despair you never even saw, whose despair you might have helped, but you never saw it, whose despair you might have used, but you never tried.*

A fool who could have so easily been deceived, said Alan.

A fifty-year-old you could have knocked down, said Valeria.

Cassie said, *You ended my life, too*; she was in tears. Her face suddenly presenting itself to mine, the horrible weeping of suffering without control and without hope; I didn't want to look at it. So I put my hands over my eyes but even so they were all visible: Cassie rocked back and forth in pain; Lori read her book; Cass cried out loud, *Oh Nath, Nath, what has she done to me? I'm so lonely!* and fell to her knees, her chiton spreading out on the rock, her hair stirring about her face, one lock drifting up and back, up and back, and she throwing her arms out in a cross, as if quartering the circle she was part of, dropping her mouth open, staring outwards in the stupor of utter despair.

Nath got up. She stepped out of the circle — and oh, how that shocked me! — and lifted her blazing-white face, wringing her hands together but not at all like someone suffering; rather she was exercising the joints and the bones, locking her fingers together and pulling, like an athlete limbering up, like a violinist getting ready to play, like a fighter going into the ring. She said:

Starving? You've been starving all your life. What do you know about it, you with your petty religion and your baby's politics, thinking you could change the world! You are an arrogant, vile, unimportant woman.

Silence. They're all speaking at once. They're silent. They all have the same voices. They're running out of words.

You incompetent bitch, she said, *what else can you do but die? It's the only thing you're good at. Exiled to this place? It was made for you; if it hadn't existed, you would have created it. When you were born, there was no real place for you, no one was fond of you, not really, not of that real self only you knew, so you took the whole world on your back and put yourself in the center of it and said It's mine and said I'm going to get everything and I'm going to change everything. And when it didn't work you ran away, and when that didn't work you started starving yourself to death but slowly, slowly, with lectures you didn't like and friends you didn't know any more and when that didn't work you wanted to die but you wouldn't leave us alone, not you, you wanted company; so you killed Alan and you killed John and you killed Lori and you killed Cassie and you killed Val and you killed me.*

Look at yourself, she said. *Look at your fear. Look in my face and you'll see your own rage and your own deprivation. I know you. Do you think I don't know you?*

Look in the mirror.

They didn't fade. They got sharper and sharper, exactly as I had seen them last. They walked out of the cave without touching one another, as if they had no feelings for each other and no relation to each other: Val went first and John Ude second, then Alan, with none of his beauty left, and Nathalie, without any expression on her face, and then Cassie, with as commonplace a look as if nothing had happened. They stepped out into the sunshine and I think they may have turned to one side or the other on the little ledge that's in front of the cave, but I don't know. They just disappeared. Then Lori came, dragging her book, and her other hand in her father's: Victor Graham in his beautiful, blue dress-suit, not as he had looked when he died, but spruce, rich, handsome, even smiling. He looked free.

He said, 'They do go on, don't they? But we all have something like that.' Lori was intently shaking the dust off her fairy-tale book. He said, a little apologetically, 'She likes that kind of thing. You know? And I'm told it's a good book. Come on, dear,' and he started towards the entrance to the cave. I noticed with a kind of horror that he had to bend over because he was such a tall man; the roof was too low for him. At the threshold he stepped out as if he were going to continue walking right out into space, and as he began to dissolve in the sunshine – or I lost sight of him because my eyes weren't used to the dazzle outside – Lori tugged at his hand for a moment and turned back. She said something to me and then she went out with her father into that brilliancy I couldn't see, and was gone. I have never seen that child so well-mannered.

She smiled at me dutifully.

Then she said, 'Thank you.'

'For what?' I said. She looked surprised.

She said, 'For killing me.'

★

103

Nothing settled. Nothing! What's inside my head comes out, that's all. Don't think I believed in them, that they could get here, that they accused me, that six people could stand up inside this cave, that they levitated out the door, that I didn't form them from the cracks and striations in the walls, the dirt, boulders, bumps, lumps, shadows, that stuff.

Anyhow she was only being polite to please her father.

Afternoon. L. B. came to visit, much more realistically, by the way, sitting cross-legged against the side wall and shifting around uncomfortably, sticking his tongue out a little when the pebbles hurt his ass. There were even footprints coming in from the ledge outside, I mean places where his feet had disturbed the cave floor; at least for a while there were. I was so pleased to see him, so glad, but I didn't dare touch because I knew he'd go. So I asked him why didn't he bring the contra-tuba he'd left outside the cave.

He said, 'Are you kidding? The silly thing's *enormous*. Think of all the ectoplasm it would take. Besides, you know I can't play it.'

I got snide and made an improper suggestion about something else he couldn't play in his present state.

He blushed, mostly in his delicate ears, where you could always see it happen; he has wonderful ears, slightly transparent, that always reminded me of a bat's, they stick out like two silky signal flags; he said, 'Oh dear, no, really you shouldn't,' which is exactly the way L. B. has always talked.

I said, 'Well, what are you doing now? Still preaching? Still teaching? Are you asleep somewhere and visiting me in your sleep?'

Silence. He looked at the floor. He seemed very unhappy. That twist of the head, putting his chin into the hollow of his collarbone. Hunching up the shoulder. Rubbing his cheek and his shoulder as he always did when he suffered, ol' knobbly man, and now he's doing something else, something rather distressing; he looks up and there are tears running out of his wide blue eyes.

I cried, alarmed, 'Elbee, are you *dead*?'

Silence. The erotic is going out of him like water out of a glass; once I saw someone nearly sever a finger when I was working in hospital and the color went out of his face like a column of mercury dropping; that doctor turned from brown to greyish-brown as if somebody'd pulled down a shade. L. B. is doing this, and he's getting flatter and flatter somehow, sharper and sharper, like an image that's alive but doesn't quite belong with its background. I don't like this.

He said, 'Oh my dear, you've committed murder.'

'Go away.' (I said it again, totally shocked: 'Go away!')

'But my dear, how can I love you if you've committed murder?'

I started to cry. 'Yes,' I said, 'all right, you Christian, don't.'

I added, 'You know it was self-defense!'

He merely looked at me.

'Of course it was, of course it was!' I said. 'You saw it. I mean, if you're made of ectoplasm and all. I mean running into the brush yelling Colonize, Colonize, and all that. They were going to force me to have babies. I was going to be tied to a tree and raped, for goodness' sake. It was a mass-delusional system, L. B., you know what they're like, and anybody who doesn't agree has to be shut up somehow because it's too terrifying. So I ran away, but they wouldn't let it be; they came back after me to drag me back into that insanity and I killed them; I had to. I kept telling them we were all dead. You know that. And we were. I bet they had a lot more fun chasing me than they would have had by dying slowly in a few months. It gave them something to do. And I might remind you, old buddy, that several of those nice people were trying to kill me.'

'Murderer,' he said.

I started crying again. I said, 'You get out of here, you father! You just get out of here! This is not your cave so you just haul ass!'

He said thoughtfully, 'Murder. Pure murder. Don't you think? And for no reason. Just because those people annoyed you. You assumed, of course, that they ought to adapt to you; it never occurred to you that you ought to adapt to them. You simply didn't like them.'

I couldn't talk.

He said, 'Out of spite, really, I think. Don't you? A hidden wish. Anger. The chance to do what you'd always really wanted to do. I think what you always wanted, under the camaraderie, under the sociability, was the chance to be really and truly alone, autocratically alone, one might say. Arrogantly alone. Yes, that's right. You talk so much about there being no law here for the others, but I don't think you ever reflected truly that, after all, there was no law binding you, either, nothing to keep you from ultimately doing exactly what you wanted to do. And what was it? Why, to kill. One might look at the whole series of events as a series of provocations; you see, you pushed them to the point where they'd give you a pretext for murdering them and then when Nathalie nagged them into following you – it was she who did it, of course; if Nathalie had been more intelligent and a little less conventional, and hadn't needed people around to boss so much, I think she would have done exactly what you did – well, you're very like Nathalie, you know. Very like. Probably the only person in history to depopulate an entire planet so easily. Pocket genocide, one might call it. And for spite. For sheer nastiness and bad feeling. And for no other reason. So I can hardly love you now, can I?'

I got to my feet, although I was dizzy and shaking – oh, was I shaking! – and I cried, *You liar! You fake! Why are you here? Why'd you bother to come? You never loved me, never, never, you only pretended and then you fake things up because you know it wasn't like that and it's all just to destroy me!*

He said calmly, 'That is true.'

Then you're the killer! and I screamed, I really did. There was more argument running in and out of my ears, pro and contra, not a loud booming or even a sound but pure confusion until I couldn't tell if I were speaking or not or he was or not; it was all a tangle.

So I leaned over to hit him and fell on my face. I don't think falls can hurt me now, I'm too light. Anyway, there was a sort of cushiony, dreadful mess of arguing and pullings-apart and past lives all over the floor; I think that helped. And my own blood sounding in my ears. By looking up I could see L. B.'s face close to mine and though it was the same face, it wasn't, not really; it had become unchangeable, like a photograph. A photograph of a smile is a smile first but look at it too long and it comes apart into tics and muscular oddities; soon you can't even tell if it's a smile or not. The time element has been left out. L. B. was like that. I think he was gloating, but I couldn't tell. He might have been smiling. He might have been sad. He was going to do something very bad and it would make him happy. Then I knew it wasn't L. B.

He said, *God hates you.*

Now that's ridiculous. It's abominably silly and it would never cross L. B.'s mind, let alone his lips, except as a particularly comic, blasphemous horror. This is someone else.

I said carefully, 'How do you know?'

He said with a sickly-sweet smile, 'I know what you know.'

I said, 'But how, L. B.? How do you know? Are you my conscience?'

'Yes,' he said, edging along the wall as if he wanted to get out of the cave without getting to his feet. 'Yes, I'm your conscience.'

'Come on, L. B.,' I said. 'You're not my conscience.'

'I'm not your conscience.'

'Tell me,' I said in, I think, a kind of croak because everything was breaking up very fast now and oh, I had to be cunning or I would have to live with this monster for the rest of my life, for eternity, who knows, I said, 'Tell me, tell me, where is L. B. right now?'

'Don't know,' he said.

'Are you L. B.?' I said, and suddenly still, he assumed an even odder, intense kind of fixity — yet this one was totally human — like the moment when someone touches you on the shoulder from behind and you don't know who; you gather your forces internally, perhaps, or do what's called 'holding your breath' though it's more like holding your mind, not thinking. The strict arrest. I'm not sure I want to find out who this is.

He said pathetically, 'I try. I do try. Please believe me.'

'Who are you?'

'You give me such an awful role to play. That's because you're such an awful person. You're most unfair.'

'Now look here, you idiot —'

'Yes, I'm an idiot. *You're* an idiot! Making poor Elbee into your conscience and what a conscience! It's just like you. Of course he never loved you. Who could? You're not loveable. *I* don't love you. Nobody could ever love you. Why? Because you're bad, bad, bad, bad, bad —'

and was talking to myself. Had been. All along. Of course. Unmistakeably sincere. To think as badly of him as that!

But I am. I'm impossible. Dreadful. Totally wretched little bit of nothing. He should have dropped me long ago.

What I could have

Should have

Couldn't

Should have thought really

Really! Arrogant, solitary, secretly cruel, I am. I am. Used to say to myself Who isn't, who isn't, but it's not true. I've been unhumanly hungry and starved for years, as nasty as a starved rat. A cannibal. Wished they wouldn't be persuaded. And glad they weren't. Give it a good end, go out in a great big bang. End to stupid parties after lectures, people I didn't know, people I wanted to kick, trying to live without roots like an air plant, endless traveling with idiots, trying to pretend they're bright when I'd like to hit them and I like them when I don't and it doesn't matter when it does and I ought to love that hateful, ghastly bunch and oh Lord, what was I *doing* there, anyhow.

I rather enjoyed killing them off and I don't care. Except Cassie.

Alan-Bobby hit in the head with a rock, *good for him*! Nathalie shot? *Good for her!* John Ude shot, *good*. Lori, *fine*. Val, *best of all*. Goody good good for *them*! It's a game they understood inside-out and once I started playing I rather liked it because I'm not exactly an amateur, either, you understand, and its all yummy self-assertion, all big adventure, isn't it, oh my, creeping about in the canebrake in our under-drawers, trying to pot each other.

No, I had to. I really had to.

But all the same I did. What, 'pocket genocide'? I guess so. Up to the elbows in blood. Poetry.

And now I have to live with this awful, awful woman, this dreadful, wretched, miserable woman, until she dies.

I cried myself to sleep – not real tears, silly, easy tears; the awful thing was that I couldn't stop, they're the kind that keep leaking out of you – and I called myself all sorts of insulting names. I fell asleep calling myself names. Dreamed we were back together at my place, all this sensuality a topography I couldn't describe to you, a sort of lovely pocket universe, and in the summer dawn (this really happened once) from some dingy cement ledge outside our window:

SQUEEEEEEEECH!

Like a siren right under your pillow. The damnedest sound. The bed quaked. I thumped him in the ribs, said, 'Bang on the wall.' He said, I think sitting up, 'What? What?'

I said, 'Sparrows. Bang on the wall.'

There was a nest in the air-conditioner. It was an old portable and made a beautiful bird's-nest, right between the ledge and the bottom of the exhaust, a lovely steady current of warm air. Tremendously attractive. If you'd been able to go outside, you'd have seen grass and twigs sticking up haphazardly from beneath the machine. Sparrows are messy builders. If you whop at them, they shut up for a couple of minutes, just enough to get back to sleep.

SQUEEEEEE-HEEEEECH!

By then he was up. Quivering. He said, 'Kill them.'

I sat up. 'Why? They're just babies.'

'Babies? They're banshees.'

'Look, the building people are coming in a week to close up the gap. They'll be flying and out by then. You don't want to murder a whole bunch of helpless little cutey baby birds, now do you?'

'Yes,' he said.

I said, 'Um . . . I know, but you can't take the unit out; I tried. Takes special tools. And you need a cable through the hook on top or the whole unit falls eighteen stories and murders someone.'

The food factory was at it again. Oh God, it *was* awful.

I said, 'Elbee, have respect for the sanctity of life.'

'*Sparrows?*' he said.

And sparrows they were. Every sunrise the infants woke and screamed horror and starvation – you have no idea what that is like only a meter from your ear and no soundproofing – and opened their tiny, little, red beaks: *feed me! feed me!* (at about one hundred and sixty degrees' extension) and drove their desperate parents, who probably wanted to sleep as much as I did, out to exhaust themselves and ruin their health finding enough polluted insects to cram thrice its own weight each day into that insatiable scarlet gullet. There is nothing – I repeat, *nothing* – in the homeothermic realm uglier or stupider than a baby bird. And sparrows! The only flying specie nobody's ever had to re-seed or protect or re-transport or do anything but discourage. If they'd been swallows or cranes or titmice, anything. Even grackles. But sparrows? They're taking over the world.

SQEEE-HEEEEE-HEEEEE-HEEEEEEEEECH!

'Oh God, have you been living with that?' he said.

I said yeah, well, at least they matured fast. Then he began to look as if he were getting dangerous ideas – dangerous to himself, I mean – like attempting to open the top of the window or unscrew the front of the conditioner and try to poke through the coils.

They did it again. He pounded on the wall. 'Shut up, you bloody birdies!' Silence. We had slept two hours. I usually wadded the extra pillow over my head and managed somehow. L. B. shouted, 'Filthy, lousy, bird-brained birds!' He was always accurate. And added, 'Oh, why couldn't you have had the sense to be born fledermausen?'

We liked bats.

Then he said, 'Oh hey, do you have a rubber hose? If we could pry some of the insulation off and run a hose through the edge –'

'And pipe them ten thousand worms?' I said. 'Oh no. They'll stop in an hour, honestly.'

He said, hopefully, 'Boiling water?'

I shook my head. 'I tried.' The trick is to get at them when they're first nesting and repeatedly scare the living daylights out of them – birds are very emotional – until they get the idea there's a large, very irritable, dangerous mammal who comes with the site and they do, finally, go somewhere else. But once they've laid eggs, it's you or them. And I hate them. Nesting in my ear. Denouncing us. Making everything in your nervous system fire off all at once when you're peacefully asleep, as if you'd been electrocuted. We discussed various avicidal methods, each worse than the last, for the next hour until the clamor, no din, no – the *screams* – died down, and then we lay down again. I said, 'Oh, what a mess there'll be when they clean out the window.' And then (and I knew I was dreaming, but my dream continued to follow that scenario of twelve years ago) I prodded LB's velvety-bony rib. He gave a sleepy, chuckling gasp: harpf. Hoopf.

'Hey,' I said, 'hey, Elbee, what would you do if it was people?'

Hapf. Sometimes he felt like a moose in bed: all antlers.

'Really,' I said, 'what?'

'Kill'm.' Pwft.

'No, if it was people, if they bothered you more than that, if they really wanted to . . . to put you in jail forever or mess your life up or something, I don't mean kill you but something really bad, what would you do?'

An adult bird twittered softly outside: there, there, my lovely little red-funnel darlings, my yelling stomachs, my squally, pin-feathered dearies, my hope, my joy.

Damn them! Parental insanity.

I woke up.

Twelve years ago I'd gone to sleep and so missed the answer that way. A classic, textbook dream but so far, so very, very far, so unfortunately far away from any textbook at all.

I'll tell you the neo-Christian theory of love. The neo-Christian theory of love is this:

There is little of it. Use it where it's effective.

Then I started to cry again but too easy, just leaking out of my soul, almost comfy. Penance can't be like that. And then I thought of Nathalie, Alan, Val, & Co., all fledglings in a nest, all flopping about and squeeching like mad: oh feed, feed, feed! Agree! Agree! Agree!

I *am* arrogant. Dreams don't lie. Can't do it in a dream. It made me laugh. I'll never be properly guilty, can't be, it's too funny.

Feed me, feed me, feed me! (Am I one, too?)

Read me, read me, read me!

Marilyn came, not in a dream or vision, but just a fragrance I couldn't see beyond the edge of the ledge. Night. The Smudge rising. When there are no stars you see the sky differently: huge, immense, utter Nothing if there's any light, then flat and right against your eyes when it's black. You imagine walls, as if it were a room. She was visiting. You know? I imagined talking to her. Can't remember, except a general feeling it was all right. Marilyn talking silently, ever so eloquent gestures. Like the alphabet for the deaf with her hands but so beautifully tender: *One* and she opposed her right forefinger to the third finger of her left hand: *Two* and it was third finger to third finger; *Three* and it was fourth to the same third, left-hand finger; *Around* and she rotated both hands, fingers loosely half-curled like a shell; *Together* and she joined one palm to another, spread fingers to spread fingers, like mirror meeting mirror. Her lips moving. Head to one side, perhaps wry, perhaps smiling. Bending her head to take off her big glasses: behold naked Marilyn! She touched lightly the collar of her shirt: another difficult curve, this one half-closing, flatter, fingers together but thumb apart. What fine points she was making. I watched her until sunrise, slept, dreamed of L. B. playing in an orchestra (ah, but he played *le jass* on the side, L. B. skulking into magical romantic cellar at midnight with infra-tuba, plugging self

into huge console in middle of smoke, tilting hat over face for *flics*,
slurping beer, blowing tuba, making wicked and forbidden sounds
from current in brain, sneer on face, hat tipping up and down,
shoulders bouncing, nope, friend-o, I just do this for amps, great
screams, *les cops!* and off we go into the night, no L. B. but only
infra-tuba-with-legs and blushing ears going skrimble skramble
down cobbled pavement into romantic darkness and falling flat on
face) and when he took off his traditional, somber, musician's
black tights with silver-sparkle round the wrists, neck, and ankles,
and he said – peering at crotch level – 'What is this?' and I 'What
is that?' and we cried out together, 'Love!' and danced naked but
very classically, until he got down on one knee and I went up on
point on his unpadded thigh, bracing myself against his bony
shoulder, doing an arabesque, and he said, 'Must you?' and then he
said, 'Really, you'd better wake up; that hurts,' and he added,
'Why are you dreaming in French? It's not like you.'

I woke up laughing.

Day. Day something. Something from Marilyn stays about, something from L. B. I'm dreadfully thin. I mean in the ordinary way,
of course, not starving yet because starving takes too long, I think.
It takes months. That's amazing. Can see not only my ribs, which
I always could, more or less, but also the bones around my knees
and my thighs have got all flappy. Arms, too. Does that signify
anything? My thumb and middle finger meet round my upper
arm. I sat in the water and thought: should I measure myself?
(Being delightfully dirty; you can shit in the water, first of course
sitting in it and backing it up, and eventually you'll be clean all by
itself. I get dizzy standing.) Only maybe this is an hallucination,
too: skinny legs, big knees, hanging belly, something left over
from a newsreel. Well, I'm not swollen up. Can't remember what
that's called, with the no-protein. Or is that only with children?
Different when you're grown up.

I don't know.

A couple of times I tried to see my face in the water. I mean I think I did. But now doesn't matter, I'm just being, the most extra-ordinary freedom just to be behind your face and not cultivate it as if it were a house plant. 'Cheeeeez!' Me at five, fidgeting in the holo studio, fancying the cameras are dental machines and I'm being ter-ribly brave. Less boring than just waiting. Earlier today there was lots of music coming from all over, which was a terrific liberation; it's all been sealed up inside me till now and I doubt somebody strung up wires and speakers all over the cacti. You don't need them if you've a good memory. I went slowly to the ledge and hung my feet over, feeling like the Old Herb Lady who lives in the cave; it was coming from all around, in this strange place, like a vast, inhuman auditorium, Bach from the hills and bushes and when I looked into the blazing blue sky, Handel. Very appropriate.

The trumpet shall sound!

I wonder if they really believed that. Et cetera. The trumpet shall and we shall, et cetera. My singing must sound awfully squeaky and the vocoder isn't set for music; this will just be words. It was memory-music but I had no control over it, it just came, what I've lectured about for years and loved for years, like Saint Francis preaching to the birds (except sparrows); here I am playing music for silver-haired plants and alien hills. They all sat in rows and listened. From the organ (which? brain? kidney? lung?) Bach's Toccata and Fugue in D Minor, which if you don't know it, I'm sorry for you. A great, majestick, howling discord that grumbles down into the abyss and then insists its way stubbornly up again, bigger than a building, bigger than anything; to play it properly you'd need a speaker the size of a cathedral. A throat as big as the Mississippi. It played and played; everything I knew played until I wept, how can one not? If there's faith, there's music. They whisper:

Since by Man came death . . .

(heh heh that leaves me out, even in the minor key, pianissimo)

Since by Man came death . . .

(more insistent now, and heavier, but they still believe it)

BY MAN CAME ALSO! THE RE-SUR-RECTION!

(wups, fast and fortissimo and major; I think they mean it)

And they played and they sang and I wept, everything I ever knew, for Baroque music is keyed into Isaac Newton's kind of time; it's the energy of that new explosion of philosophic time: perspective, mathematics, instant velocity, the great clock, the great wheel, harmonies, the Great Godly Grid.

Then the bushes whispered in succulent German O my heart, my heart. Out of my big griefs. My little songs. Inching towards Einstein. Let me love, Mother, let me lean on his bosom. I thought the frost-flowers on the windowpane meant Spring . . .

Over here the Phoenix Reaction and God as Engineer. Over here entropy, suffering, death. And then the real Einstein, too complicated for me although I know what I'm supposed to like, Stravinsky and after; it makes my head ache, referring to things in all dimensions and sometimes backwards. And then it turns primitive, this is a bloody great dynamo and this a laboring flute. And then music-as-theatre. And round again. Round and round.

All the music in the world says all the things in the world — I mean the universe, of course — and that's everything there is.

So it all cancels out.

Sound the trumpet!

It is.

And let the listening hills rejoice.

They are.

I started up The Messiah but you have to be quite careful about *Every valley* because I'm near one and it might get ideas; I mean *shall be exalted* and there we go with an X-quake.

Well, if it all goes round, it's a spiral anyway — a four-dimensional one ('hyper-spiral') or like that theory of the four cosmi bongling into each other perpetually like ping-pong balls — matter with 'forward' time, matter with 'backward' time, antimatter with 'forward' time, antimatter with 'backward' time, only I think that would take five dimensions (six? seven? seventeen?) no, only three and Time, and you have to have ideal Ping-Pong balls because they never damp out. I like the older way better because I'm irresponsible: forever and ever. Forever and ever.

Forever and ever!

Hallelujah, hallelujah, hallelujah, hallelujah, hallelujah, hallelujah, hallelujah, hallelujah! Forever and ever.

Quite a trick, for someone who doesn't believe in God.

Only Handel always makes me cry so. The people who walk in darkness, those who dwell in the land of the shadow of death, they all do a lot of crying.

Day. Sometime. I looked up and, you know, it wasn't surprising, there's another piece of my past come back; I am really not quite sure if this is another hallucination or only a memory, but at my knee at this moment there is a five-year-old little girl standing in grey trousers, red cloth shoes, and a blue cotton polo shirt. Wearing what the gilded youth of Empire would have worn on the playing fields a hundred and sixty years ago. More or less. She is the only child I ever knew who was named after an airport.

I said, 'Kennedy?'

No answer. She died in a car crash years ago but Marilyn lived. Marilyn's her mother. Three months in hospital: broken ribs, a broken arm, concussion, two operations on her knees, broken bones in her face.

Kennedy died twenty minutes after the crash. She was unrecognizable. I mean they could tell who she was only by her size; there was another child, someone else's, in the car, and Marilyn had another daughter. The other child wasn't hurt, only bruised. The inflation bags didn't open for some reason: people thrown about the inside of a steel can. They had to cut the car open.

She's put her hand on my knee. But I can't feel it.

Silence. I said, 'Kennedy, you were quite obnoxious when you were alive. You were a screamer. You used to steal my needle and scissors to fight beasts with when you visited. You lifted up your voice and complained and when I took them back, you kicked me.'

Silence. She has no expression. Not grave, not gay. Interested, perhaps? No, she's only looking at me.

'Have you come to get me?' I said.

Silence. That same almost intent – yet not intent – gaze.

She must have something to tell me. Otherwise why come all that way? If she had lived two weeks longer she would have gone from daycare to school and she was rather proud of that because she was one of the very few children (the only elegance she could parade) who had a single mother and not eight mothers or five dads or a mix of mothers and dads or two dads or three mothers, and she was great friends with a little boy named Harold, who had a single father.

'Where's Harold?' I say to her.

Silence. She was anxious, rather obsessed with growing up, very fierce in defending her rights, and her death nearly killed her mother.

I tried. 'Marilyn –'

She put her hand again on my knee and this time I felt it, a thrill, a fear, a warning, that insistent, communicating, hot-damp, little hand.

A gateway. A sign. A messenger. Though nothing's settled. Fill in all the standard things about living being dying and the questions making the answers, everyone's dying all the time, dying is life, &c., &c. But I still don't know anything.

This is not Kenny, who is drifting towards the door of the cave without a backward glance at me, like the night Marilyn was brought into hospital and I kept seeing her standing between two rooms, a lit one and a dark one, but they were both empty. Turning softly and vaguely from one to the other, and both empty. I still don't understand that. I mean, both empty.

Kenny was always so fierce in life: squinch lines around her eyes, thin mouth either distended or twisted, cheeks blown out with rage, sucked in for gloom. She was never still; you could never measure the proportions of her face.

I guess I ought to follow her out, throw myself over the cliff. Can't, though. I'd only roll down like an idiot or a thistle and get impaled on something; I can't jump any more. I've printed out most of this and put it in the tin box; I'm wearing the rest of it around my neck. Pushed the box into the back cave wall because it's going to fall soon. I mean in a few hundred years or so, sometime, it's clear it will.

The splendid sun out there, lighting up the world. The lit room. The empty room.

I will record a few last words, try to think of something significant, and since after that concert — everything's ringing still — there's not much else to do. I mean. I mean I will not. Since I don't care. Thank God it's over. Odd to look back and see how much should have been changed, but one forgets the everydayness of it and the reasons why; I don't suppose I did better with the room than most or worse or whatever. I mean if they make you rent it unfurnished, you see.

An afterlife: that would be nice, I suppose.

No. Better not.

Time. Time to go. Which way: instant, euphoric, religious, sleep, trancelike — really, nowadays you'd think one was shopping for couch covers. I think I'll leave them all behind, pity not to get to the real thing at last after all this trouble. I can muster up a jump. I can roll off the cliff, maybe bump my head, maybe die of thirst; lots of delirium, dirty my pants, interesting stuff, my whole past or something. The natural method.

I'm going to do a joke; I will put as the last words on this, Oh I see people in uniforms coming through the brush downstream; someone's coming to rescue me, Goddam.

And there they are! Coming through the brush — almost at the horizon, I think, but in white — people in white, as if they were the survey team for this tagged, unfurnished house — and they're following the line of the river. Six of them. Coming this way. What a damned nuisance, I will have to be alive again, how exasperating.

Bet you believed it.

Told you, joke.

Can't remember worrying about this. This dying. Can't remember. Why? Will put the print-out away, wait for the hill to bury it, and keep the vocoder. Such immense kindness from the hill. Nice hill. Nice sun (setting behind a bush someplace). So friendly, all this strange world, really. Walls. Floor. Astonishingly put together.

I've done it. But kept the vocoder. And I have to be near the box or you won't find it. Whoever you are. It's the loneliness, really. Marilyn still alive somewhere, that's the ghastly thing. I'll do it the instant way, I suppose, just to be finished with it. Get it all over, all that dying. Long dying: long, long dying, forty-two years, that's too much and I really *wish*

If only I can get into it right, fit right. You know. I've got the ampoule in my hand, only have to break it. Skin contact.

> *Death, thou shalt die*
> *The City of Dreadful Night*
> *Eternity as a bath house full of spiders* (but he was nuts)
> *The Celestial City*
> *Gehenna*
> *History is a nightmare from which humanity longs to awaken*
> *Death is not part of life; death is not lived through* (I'll buy that)
> Got this thing in my hand. OK

well it's time

PENGUIN WORLDS

Classic science fiction introduced by brilliant contemporary novelists

Science fiction is a genre that gives us gripping plots and fantastical creations. It is also a genre that challenges us with fresh ideas about all kinds of things – politics, philosophy, technology – how the world works and what it means to be human. The Penguin Worlds project celebrates this incredible range, richness and invention, taking the very best from the twentieth century science fiction canon.

This series includes prescient environmental dystopia, a pioneering example of early cyberpunk, classic urban fantasy, chilling short fiction, and one of the most influential voices in feminist science fiction. Each one is a groundbreaking classic of its day; Penguin is proud to bring these classics to a whole new generation of readers.

Penguin Worlds is curated by Hari Kunzru and Naomi Alderman.

Hari Kunzru is the bestselling author of *The Impressionist* and *Transmission*. His new novel, *White Tears*, is published by Penguin in 2017.

Naomi Alderman is the acclaimed author *Disobedience, The Lessons* and *The Liars' Gospel*. Her latest novel, *The Power*, is published by Penguin in 2016.